DEMON HUNTERS
ASCENSION

OLIVIA CHASE

LITTLE, BROWN BOOKS FOR YOUNG READERS
www.lbkids.co.uk

LITTLE, BROWN BOOKS FOR YOUNG READERS

First published in Great Britain in 2017 by Hodder and Stoughton

1 3 5 7 9 10 8 6 4 2

A CIP catalogue record for this book
is available from the British Library.

ISBN 978-0-349-00228-6

Printed and bound in Great Britain by
Clays Ltd, St Ives plc

The paper and board used in this book are made
from wood from responsible sources.

MIX
Paper from
responsible sources
FSC® C104740

Little, Brown Books for Young Readers
An imprint of
Hachette Children's Group
Part of Hodder and Stoughton
Carmelite House
50 Victoria Embankment
London EC4Y 0DZ

An Hachette UK Company
www.hachette.co.uk

www.hachettechildrens.co.uk

With special thanks to Rosie Best

To Karen, Kate and Becca

PROLOGUE

Wednesday November 16th, 11:42 p.m.,
Café Lamarck, Paris

The fog coiled in the streets of Paris like a living thing. It shrank back from the street-lights and clawed deep into the dark corners of the city. It lay heavy on the waters of the Seine and pooled in the steep, narrow streets of Montmartre, swallowing up whole neighbourhoods. Cars crept along the roads with their headlights on full blast, and lost tourists huddled in the bars, hoping that the fog would lift in the morning.

Eva Moreau knew that it wouldn't.

Leaning in the shadow of a huge stone doorway near the Cathédrale de Saint-Denis, Eva zipped her leather jacket up to her chin. She folded her arms, shielding

1

herself from the chill and from the creeping shudder that kept crawling up her spine.

Every instinct she had was telling her that she needed to get this done, and quickly. If she was wrong, then the search would have to begin again, but if she was *right* . . .

She *was* right. It couldn't be a coincidence. She didn't have time for it to be a coincidence. Even as she stood in the street, the fog seemed to close in on her, to sniff around her like a hungry dog.

Sate your hunger somewhere else, demon, she thought. *There's nothing for you here.*

Did she feel the presence in the fog turn away, or was it all in her mind? If the demon truly came for her, would bluster be enough to save her life?

Paris needed a Trinity, and soon.

She watched the eerie-coloured shadows that filtered through the fog from the windows of a corner café. A warm yellow light spilled out on to the street as the door opened. Eva heard the muffled rattle of drums and guitars from inside, and the wail of a saxophone. Then voices:

'Oh balls, it's cold out here. Franci, hurry up!'

'Yeah, hold on . . . '

The two girls were dark spots in the fog, like shadow puppets against the café's light. If she hadn't known them by their voices, Eva would have had no problem identifying them by their silhouettes: Coralie Dumas was short and svelte, her hair puffed out around her head like the seeds of a dandelion. Francine Lambert was taller, curvy, her hair falling down to the small of her back.

Eva smiled to herself as she watched them.

Coralie and Francine had known each other since before they were born. Their mothers were lifelong friends, and had attended the same doctors' surgeries and pre-natal classes. They had given birth in adjoining hospital rooms, their extended families gathered around them, celebrating this wonderful double event – two childhood friends having babies on the same day.

For Eva, who'd been eighteen years old and a second cousin of Coralie's mother, and for Francine and Coralie's mothers and grandmothers, the births had been even more of a reason to celebrate.

Born on the same day, to mothers who wielded the powers of their foremothers and bore the purple mark on their wrists: these girls would be Demon Hunters.

'You know Lea, from the family who lives in that little town in the Alps?' Eva's mother had said to Coralie's grandmother. *'She's having a baby today too. But it's a boy! Such a disappointment.'*

'What about the other families?' Coralie's grandmother had asked, biting her nails. *'Have any of them replied to your letters?'*

'Only to say there are no baby girls expected today,' said Eva's mother. *'But fate finds a way. If they are meant to be a Trinity, they will find a third. Perhaps some girl will be born early, or late, or to some forgotten line on the other side of the world. There is no reason to worry. Fate always finds a way.'*

Coralie bounced on the balls of her feet as Francine stood in the doorway of the café, hand on hip, looking down at the glowing rectangle of her phone.

'Come on, let's go,' Coralie said. 'I don't like this fog. Eva thinks it's creepy.'

Francine laughed, and put her phone away. 'Eva thinks everything is creepy. Got his number though,' she said smugly, thrusting her hands into the pockets of her coat.

'You did not!' Coralie gasped.

'Swear to God, he's just texted me, and I wasn't even out of the door.'

They started to walk away, and Eva stepped forward. She turned.

'Henri, it's time,' she said. 'Go.'

The teenager who emerged from the shadows behind her hesitated. 'Do you really think . . . ?'

Eva smiled again, despite the cold and the ache in her spine that insisted there was a demon nearby. She took Henri's hand in her own, giving it a reassuring squeeze.

'I really do. Fate always finds a way. Now go.'

Henri took a deep breath and ran their hands through their hair, sweeping its burgundy waves back from their face. 'OK.'

They set off down the road at a loping stroll, and Eva followed behind slowly, staying far enough back to be blurred from the girls' view by the fog, but watching Henri intently as they waved and called out.

'Hey, Coralie, Francine.'

'Oh, hi Henri!' Francine's arms stretched wide and she hugged Henri, standing on tiptoe to kiss them on the cheek as soon as they were within reach.

'You heading home? Wanna walk with us?' Coralie asked. She linked her arm with Henri's, and so did

Francine. They headed towards the cathedral square, past an open space where the fog wound between carefully tended trees and neat, raised beds of grass.

Eva carefully stepped after them, listening to them chatter. 'Franci's just got another boy's number. Shame we couldn't stay, she could have gone for the record.'

'Coralie is exaggerating, as usual,' said Francine.

Henri laughed. Eva thought probably only she could hear the nervous edge in their voice. 'How many would you have to get to beat your personal best?'

'Eight,' said Francine proudly, tossing her hair back. 'Ten if you count screennames. That was at a festival though; I'm never going to beat that. Or see any of those guys again. Half of them weren't even French.'

'Wow,' said Coralie. 'It's like there's just . . . nothing. You can barely even make out the cathedral.'

Coralie's train of thought had a tendency to jump the tracks, but in this case, her logic wasn't hard to follow – the three teenagers had reached the edge of the cathedral square. As she crept closer, quietly stepping between the trees to keep herself out of their line of sight, Eva saw that the square was nearly empty, and so full of fog she couldn't see the buildings on the other side. It could have stretched out for miles in front of them.

The Cathédrale de Saint-Denis loomed over their heads, little more than a dim shadow, even though they were almost close enough to touch its old, cold stones. Eva shuddered. She didn't like to come here. There were . . . *things* here, spirits that had been disturbed when they should have been left to rest and fade away. During the Revolution, the tombs had been torn open, bodies exhumed and dumped in pits of sulphur and lye to destroy every trace that they had existed. The turmoil of the dead tainted the air, made it taste strange.

Eva's mother had always said she seemed destined to be a powerful Seer, like her grandmother. But Eva had been an only child, and no others were born to any Demon Hunter family that year. Eva's Trinity had never come, yet her powers hadn't faded. Fate had wanted something different for her. She'd become Coralie and Francine's protector, their trainer and advisor, until they found their Trinity.

Paris had been without a Trinity now for forty-six years.

Too long. But not for much longer.

'How much cash do you have?' said Coralie.

'I – what?' Henri asked.

'I want coffee. He doesn't take cards.'

Eva squinted in the direction where Coralie was pointing. There was a shape in the fog, haloed by the light of a street lamp. It was a large cart, parked on the pavement under the lamp, steam rising from the taps of a gleaming black espresso machine.

'Euros? Anybody?' Coralie looked at the others.

'You don't need coffee.' Francine sniffed. 'You're the last person on *earth* who needs to be given caffeine.'

'Three coffees, please,' Henri said to the man at the coffee cart, fishing in their pockets for change.

'I'm telling you,' Francine said, tossing her hair again, 'it'll go to her tiny pixie head. You want to be the one to get her down from the ceiling, be my guest.'

'Coffee, coffee, coffee,' Coralie chanted under her breath, and Francine snorted a laugh.

'Three coffees for you, ladies,' said the man at the cart, handing the cups to the three teenagers.

'Thanks,' said Henri quietly.

The friends walked a little way from the cart and stood blowing on their steaming coffee cups.

Eva opened her mind. She tried to focus on the living, while ignoring the shuddering of the dead beneath the stone and the lurking shadow of the demonic presence. After a moment, high above, she found what she was searching for, and looked up. Perched on the cathedral, near the Rose Window, there was a huge black crow.

The clock struck midnight, and the crow took flight.

Eva reached out a hand, closed her fist on the empty air, and *caught* the crow. It dipped and whirled, fighting her control for a moment, but she held it lightly and it ceased to panic, circling through the fog, high above the three teenagers. Her fingers trembled with the effort, the short hairs on the back of her neck lifting as the invisible thread of power between her and the crow twanged and wavered, a sort of swirling feedback loop of command and reaction.

She silently opened her mouth, and the crow cawed, loud and long.

Henri, Coralie and Francine all jumped at the noise, and looked up.

The crow turned and dived at them. It folded its wings and dropped out of the fog beak-first. The teenagers shrieked and dived out of the way, shielding their faces. Coralie dropped her coffee on the ground and the scalding liquid steamed like acid on the cold stone. The crow pulled up at the last minute with a powerful flap of its enormous wings, and soared back up into the fog.

'What the hell?' Francine shook droplets of coffee off her hand.

'Where is it? Where did it go? Is it gone?' Coralie spun on the spot.

Eva brought the crow around.

'No, it's coming back! Get out of the way!'

The three of them scattered. Coralie sprang up the stone steps of the cathedral to shelter in the doorway. Francine stepped into the halo of a street lamp, scanning the sky and holding her un-spilled coffee ready to throw, like a smoking Molotov cocktail.

Henri paused, and glanced over their shoulder towards the trees where Eva was standing.

Sweat prickled on the back of Eva's neck as she turned and drove the crow down once more.

Do it, she willed Henri. *I believe. We just need to prove it.*

Henri stepped hesitantly backwards and forwards, keeping both the girls in their field of vision.

Eva knew at once when they had found the right spot, the place where the three of them formed a perfect, even-sided invisible triangle. Henri straightened up from their habitual shy slump, their shoulders pulling back, chin tilting up. The girls' posture changed, too. Eva saw Coralie's head snap up, heard her gasp *'What?'*, and saw Francine's chest rise and fall with a deep, slow breath.

Static electricity crackled between them. The last few chimes of midnight rang out, seeming sluggish and distorted. Eva drove the crow down, one more time, into the centre of the crackling triangle.

There was a burst of something across her vision, like the swirling pink and green after-effects of staring at a light bulb for too long, and control of the crow was torn away from her. She recoiled, blinking.

When her vision cleared, she saw the crow shake itself, feathers ruffling indignantly, and hop away. The three teenagers were still standing, staring at each other in amazement.

The force that quivered between them had gone – Coralie had moved first, running down the steps towards the others, pulling her coat tight around her small shoulders. Henri was rubbing their temples. Francine carefully put her coffee down on the paving stones, her hands slightly shaking.

Eva let out a laugh, high and clear and triumphant. The three teenagers jumped and looked around.

'Who's there?' Coralie shrieked.

'*Eva?*' Francine peered through the fog. 'Is that you?'

Eva walked towards them, her freezing hands in the pockets of her jacket, smiling. 'It's only me. I'm sorry for the subterfuge, girls.'

'But Eva,' Francine said, 'what does this mean? Did we just make a ... a Trinity?'

'No!' Coralie gasped. 'That's insane, that's not how it – how could – no *boy* was ever a ...' she threw her hand over her mouth. 'Oh ... Henri, I'm sorry. It's just ...'

'It's OK,' Henri said, shrugging, letting their hair fall over their face. 'Believe me, I know this is weird.'

'But, does this mean you're … *What* does this mean?' Francine gaped at Henri, open-mouthed.

Henri gave her a slightly hysterical grin. 'I don't know!'

'I do,' Eva said. She nodded at the three of them, wishing that she could share their confused happiness for Henri. But there wasn't time. 'It means Henri's a Demon Hunter. One of the true line. And it means we have a lot of work to do, and I can't train you so quickly on my own. We need someone with real experience, someone who knows what we might be fighting.'

She pulled her phone from the pocket of her jacket and tapped in a name. The phone began to ring, and the screen lit up with a single word.

Isobel.

CHAPTER ONE

Thursday November 17th, 11:56 p.m.,
the Royal Mile, Edinburgh

'Oh my God, when all the lights went off . . . '

'And it was just her in the dark . . . '

'And everyone started stamping their feet . . . '

'I thought they were going to bring the roof down, everything was shaking.' Minerva threw an arm around my shoulders, almost bearing us both down on to the sidewalk. 'Di. You are a genius. That was the best gig I've ever been to.'

I croaked a sore-throated laugh and gave her a squeeze back.

The whole Royal Mile was wreathed in fog so thick you could barely see from one street lamp to the next, and people were huddling in groups, close to the light, as if they were afraid of getting separated from the herd and picked off by wolves. The three of us half-strolled, half-staggered down the Lawnmarket, weaving to avoid the clumps of people. A group of men leered and whistled at us, and Vesta threw up her middle fingers to them as we passed.

'Oof,' said Minerva, sniffing at the collar of my jacket and recoiling. 'You really stink of beer.'

She wasn't wrong. The first beer that'd been spilled on me had been early in the evening, and the girl had clumsily tried to mop it up with napkins, and I'd been pretty annoyed. The second one was much later, the guy had laughed, and I'd been too blissed-out by the music to even care.

It had been that kind of night.

The warm-up act had been some folktronica duo called Highguard who I'd never heard of, but I'd ended up downloading both of their LPs over the venue wi-fi. Then Glass Towers had come on, and . . . wow. Kit Facet's voice, Emmaline Sharma's wild drumming, Josie Hayes on synth, Zara Basset laying down bass guitar riffs that grabbed you by the spine and wouldn't let go.

We sang along until our voices cracked. Minerva lost a shoe to the sticky floor of the venue and we had to get down on our hands and knees to find it. Vesta tripped someone who was threatening to throw his drink at Highguard, then pretended she'd had nothing to do with it. My eyeliner was smudged down my cheek, and my lipstick had long ago worn off. At some point my carefully arranged pile of ringlets had knitted into a giant tangle on top of my head. All three of us reeked of beer and sweat and onion rings.

It had been an *incredible* night.

The fog was so heavy, even for Edinburgh in the fall, that for a minute as we crossed the road on to Canongate it swallowed up the crowd outside the World's End and the three of us were left alone in a little bubble of sepia-tinted darkness. Even the sounds of the Royal Mile at kicking-out time seemed kind of muted.

'*Staaaaaaaaaay,*' Vesta crooned, imitating Kit Facet's incredible, powerful soprano. Minerva and I joined her, harmonising – or kind of. We were a little off. Actually, we were way off. With the instincts of a Trinity, we all moved on to '*in my LIIIIIFE!*' at exactly the same time, and we all changed key too. Just not to the same key.

We broke down in giggles, happy in our own little world. As we walked, Minerva got a little behind and I felt a wave of fizzing power surging through me, connecting me to the twins like an invisible, unbreakable adamantium chain. I breathed in deeply and glanced at Vesta – her eyelids had fluttered closed, and she was walking a little taller.

Whoops.

Isobel had us practise walking together so we didn't accidentally fall into a perfect triangle and set off our crackling web of power – we couldn't always tell what it would do to anything caught in our net. Plus, our Demon Hunter marks would start to glow, and having a glowing wrist tattoo in public was generally not the greatest move.

Even though in Edinburgh people usually thought we were street theatre.

For a moment, a puff of steam rose up between us and the air cleared, the tiny droplets of fog boiling away under the force of our magic. Then I laughed and rolled my shoulders, and took a few sideways steps to break formation.

'Sorry,' said Minerva, slightly slurred. 'Iss a wee problem.'

I chuckled. 'You know you get *extra* Scottish when you're drunk.'

'Ahm no drunk,' said Minerva, proving my point.

'You're such a lightweight, Minnie,' chuckled Vesta. 'You're going to regret that second pint at drills tomorrow.'

Oh God. Daily drills. I was completely sober – well, almost completely – and the mention of drills still made me shudder.

Before we moved to Edinburgh, I'd thought I was pretty fit. I was a ju-jitsu blue belt, working on getting my black. Back in London, Sensei Dave used to set us training challenges, cross-country runs around the Barbican Centre and its labyrinthine, Escher-like flights of stairs.

Compared to Isobel's Demon Hunter training, those runs were like a gentle stroll. We had running, climbing, dodging and jumping – Isobel's homebrew 1600s version of parkour – and then weightlifting, skipping rope, wrestling and weapons practice. Bizarre as it had been to be handed an ancient Japanese sword-staff as a Trinity bonding gift, my *naginata* and I were firm friends now. It felt like an extension of my own arm, and I missed it when we swapped out our own weapons for knives or clubs.

Plus, there was powers training. That meant Vesta punching holes in more and more improbably tough materials, and Minerva throwing lightning bolts at smaller and smaller targets. I would take vision-walks around Edinburgh, tracking someone by sensing their footsteps through the pavement, or laying my hands on buildings and objects and letting their history flood my mind and transport me to another time or place.

It didn't always work, and when it did, it sometimes gave me blinding headaches. But it could be amazing. I'd felt the soft fur of Greyfriars Bobby under my fingers, and seen the whole city plunged into blackness as an air raid siren wailed and the Luftwaffe's bombs came screaming down.

The best vision I'd found was something so small I'd been embarrassed to even tell Isobel about it. The University of California had an office in the city for their study-abroad students. When I ran my hand over the leaves of the potted palms in the entrance I could feel the Californian sun shining hot and clear on my face, and smell the breeze off the Pacific Ocean. The feeling of being *home* was so strong I couldn't breathe.

Of course, San Francisco hadn't been home for a long time, and I knew I wouldn't be going back any time soon. Edinburgh was home now, and I loved it like only an immigrant can.

Goddamn, it was *cold*, though.

I pulled my coat tighter around me, despite the sticky

spilled beer. Summer in Edinburgh had turned out to be bearable after all, even passably warm for a few days in August. But this cold was seriously testing me. I was wearing my heaviest coat, woollen gloves and a thick scarf, and layered tops to try to trap some heat inside, but nothing really helped. I didn't even want to think about what this place would be like in January.

'I don't understand, how are you not freezing?' I said to Vesta, who was strolling, hands in pockets, wearing only a Glass Towers T-shirt and skinny jeans under her open, billowing grey trench coat. At least Minerva had zipped her jacket up and put on a beanie hat.

'Hah! You call this cold?' Vesta said. 'Beach weather! I'm thinking about taking my coat off.'

'You're making fun of me,' I said, narrowing my eyes at her. 'Right?'

'Might be. I'm also genuinely thinking about stopping for deep-fried pizza.'

'Oh God, no,' Minerva groaned. 'I'm not having deep-fried pizza.'

'Did I say *you* were?'

I wrapped my arms around myself, my hands clamped under my armpits, and smiled to myself. It'd be time for me to leave them in a minute, to cross over the ravine and head for home and bed. Dad would probably still be up, working on his ghost-sighting app or lost in an argument on the internet. I didn't want the night to end, but at the same time, home was a pretty attractive idea right now.

I thought of the warmth of a slice of toast with too much honey, and Milly the Labrador lying down on my feet as I fell asleep. And I thought of the blissful nothingness that would come when I closed my eyes.

It'd been a couple of months since we'd defeated Witch Pricker John Kincaid: driven the demon Oriax out of his body and come really close to killing it. The moth-demon was still at large, probably looking for another victim to possess. But my recurring nightmares of darkness and knives and death's-head moths had finally stopped.

In five years, I had barely slept without having that nightmare. The first week after it stopped was like being released from prison. I slept for nearly twenty-four hours, and when I woke up I had so much energy I hardly knew what to do with myself.

I even had *dreams*, now – normal, weird dreams like the one where I was trying to vacuum the house, but when I opened the door to my room it was filled floor to ceiling with Oreos. Sometimes there were even ... nice dreams. With nice people in them. Nice people with buzz-cuts, long eyelashes, cut-glass cheekbones and tight jeans.

I hadn't seen Alex since that day with Oriax, either. Since he'd tried to kill us and we'd saved him from Kincaid's control. Since I'd flirted with him in a car park and not told the others.

I didn't know if I would ever see him again, and if I did see him, I didn't know for sure that I would be able to trust him: I really shouldn't find him popping into my mind as frequently as I did. Hell, I almost thought I could see him in the fog, in just jeans and a shirt, like he'd been when we'd met at the Solstice Festival and he'd tried to kill me. The first time.

Wait . . .

I stared harder, my heart skipping a beat.

I really could see a silhouette in the fog ahead of me. A boy. No coat. Short hair . . .

But it wasn't Alex. This boy was shorter and skinnier. As he emerged from the grey curtain, he raised his hand towards us, bare fingers clawing at the air. Something dark coated his palm, ran up his arm, dripped in viscous strings and splashed on the road.

'Oh crap,' I gasped, and threw myself forward as the boy began to stumble. I was just in time to jam my shoulder under his and take his weight as his knees went. The frozen claw of his hand clamped down on my other shoulder, smearing his blood across my front.

'I got you,' I told him. 'It's OK, I got you.'

The boy groaned as I lowered him gently to the ground. Vesta sank to her knees beside me and took hold of his bleeding arm, peering closely at the skin. Minerva stood well back, her face pale. I hoped she wouldn't throw up. She probably hoped that too.

The boy was blond and maybe a year or two younger than us. His hair was slicked to his forehead with either sweat or condensed fog, I wasn't sure which.

'We should call 911,' I told Vesta. 'There's a lot of blood.'

'Nah,' said the boy. His head rocked against my shoulder and I realised he was trying to shake it, *no*. 'Nah, not . . . not A&E. 'm fine.'

'You're not fine,' I told him. 'I'm gonna call an ambulance.'

18

'*No*. Not going,' the boy slurred, and started fidgeting, trying to push away from me and get up. 'Canna make me.'

Was he drunk? Or on the edge of passing out? He might not have been dying, but he certainly wasn't going to get anywhere by himself. Vesta and I exchanged a glance, and she held on gently but firmly to his arm.

'It's all coming from a cut across his palm,' she said. 'It doesn't look deep. He hasn't hit a vein.'

I looked, briefly. I might have been very nearly completely sober, but that didn't mean I wanted to be intimately familiar with the tear in the skin, the thick red gloop that filled the wound ...

'It's bled a lot, but it's stopping,' Vesta continued. 'Gimme your scarf.' I didn't really have any spare hands to take it off, but Vesta didn't wait for me anyway; she reached up and unwound the scarf from my neck. I shuddered as the chilly air hit my throat. She started wrapping the material around the boy's hand, so that it soaked up the slow red ooze.

I sighed. I really liked that scarf.

'Hey, you,' Vesta said, and snapped her fingers in front of the boy's face. 'Look here. Now look here.' His eyes focused on her fingers and followed as she waved them back and forth in front of him. She looked up at me and, a little worryingly, shrugged. 'If he doesn't want to go to A&E ...'

'No!' the boy groaned again.

'We can take him back to Isobel's, stitch him up there,' said Minerva, sounding slightly muffled through her fingers. 'It'll be light and warm, and we have … first-aid stuff.'

Actually, Isobel had a whole wardrobe neatly stacked with enough medical supplies to deal with almost any emergency. Not to mention the less *sciencey* supplies for the witchy remedies that she'd been trying to teach us.

I blew out a steaming breath through my teeth.

I didn't like this. But it was better than him trying to fight us or run off – he'd only hurt himself more or get the wound infected.

'I'm calling a cab,' Minerva said, phone in hand, turning away.

I turned back to the boy. His head was lolling against my shoulder, and I nudged him back upright. 'Hey,' I said. 'Don't fall asleep, or we'll take you to the ER.'

That woke him up. His eyes blinked wide open and stared at me. They were pale blue, watery and desperate.

'What's your name?' I asked him.

'Armstrong …' he muttered, then seemed to shake himself and refocus on me. 'Er. James. Ow!' He tried to recoil from Vesta as she pulled my scarf tight around his hand and tied it in a bulky knot.

'How did you hurt your hand?'

But James Armstrong just shook his head, and I didn't press him right then. He probably thought he'd get in some kind of trouble – why else would he not want to go to the emergency room?

Lights flashed through the fog. The cab was here.

'OK, time to get up now. You can do it,' I told James, although the truth was that with Vesta helping him, he didn't really have a choice. She lifted him on to his feet slowly, like she'd practised, because it tends to freak people out if you scoop them up as if they weigh less than a bag of feathers. Once he was upright, I held him there as Vesta took off her coat and wrapped it around his shoulders, hiding the worst of the blood.

Minerva waved her arms over her head and the car slowed and stopped right by us. She leaned in and gave the driver Isobel's address. The driver started plugging it into her GPS, then stopped and threw James a narrow-eyed look.

'You'll make sure your friend doesn't throw up in my cab, won't you.' It wasn't a question.

'Of course,' I said. 'He's going to be all right, he's just a bit ... overtired.'

'All right. But tell me if he goes white and I'll pull over.'

He's lost some blood – if he turns white, we might have worse problems than the floor of your cab, I thought, but I just smiled and folded James into the back seat.

'Where're we ... ' James slurred, ten minutes later, as I helped him up the steps to Isobel's front door. Vesta was already slipping her key into the lock.

'Our aunt's house,' said Minerva, wisely skipping the fifteen 'great's that technically ought to go in front of 'aunt'.

James seemed weaker now, and before we went inside I took his hand and peeked under the bloodstained scarf. But the cut was definitely only oozing, not gushing, so I pressed the material back and helped him stagger through the door.

It's funny how quickly things become normal. Not just demons and powers, training and witchy remedies – also things like hallways full of freaky taxidermied animals, their black eyes gleaming, polished claws and teeth bared. James reeled and gasped at the sight of Isobel's collection, and I remembered my own moment of horror when I'd stepped into this house for the first time. I guess it would've been kind to warn him.

'It's just taxidermy,' I said quickly. He looked at me like I was mad, but didn't resist as I steered him into the kitchen, except to lean back in bleary horror from the vulture on the stairs and the bear that loomed over the sofa.

We sat him down at the kitchen table, and he stared slack-jawed at the two taxidermy mice that held up Isobel's salt and pepper grinders. In the brighter light he seemed seriously pale, and the blood that coated his hand, arm and shirt almost seemed *too* red. I fetched warm wet towels and a tall glass of water with a few teaspoons of sugar and salt mixed in, for rehydration.

It was usually warm in Isobel's kitchen, mostly because of the antique Aga cooker she kept burning day and night – but as I passed the black iron hulk of it now it was barely radiating any heat at all.

'Where is Isobel?' I asked the twins. 'Isn't she here?'

'Er ... it's bridge night, isn't it?' Minerva said, sinking into a chair beside James.

'Wow,' I muttered. 'Go Isobel!'

The ancient Demon Hunter had been reluctant to leave her house, at least through the front door, for *decades*.

She'd been paranoid about keeping the contents of the house safe – all the books and weapons and Demon Hunter artefacts – and having met Kincaid I could vouch for her fears being pretty reasonable.

But now that Kincaid was dead, Isobel was always out and about, experiencing all the joys of modern life that a seventeenth-century witch might have missed out on.

Vesta carefully untied my scarf from James's hand, and we cleaned up the wound. It was a clean cut, right across the palm.

Minerva made James drink the whole glass of water. 'So, what happened?' she asked him, when he'd swallowed down the last of it.

'Nothing,' James said slowly. 'It was ... stupid. We were just – just hanging out. At the abbey.'

'What, Holyrood Abbey? The ruin?' Vesta raised an eyebrow. 'Open it for tourists at night, now, do they?'

James didn't answer, and Vesta nodded.

'Yeah, thought not. So what, this is from climbing the fence?'

'And that's why you didn't want to go to the ER?' I prompted. 'What about your friends? Where are they now?'

'I – I'm not ... ' James shook his head. 'It's a bit of a blur.'

I frowned. Vesta was applying a local anaesthetic cream and threading the suture needle, ready to stitch up the cut. If it was only that, James would be fine. And maybe his vagueness was just down to tiredness, adrenaline, or trying to lie about what he'd been doing.

On the other hand, I really didn't want to find myself explaining to the police, or to James's grieving family, why we hadn't taken him to hospital when we'd realised he had gaps in his memory.

There was one way I could make sure.

I slipped my hand around his, giving it a little squeeze, making out I was reassuring him and holding his palm steady for Vesta. Then I shut my eyes, and opened my mind.

I still wasn't a hundred per cent at using my powers. Just as sometimes Vesta accidentally crushed things she was only trying to pick up, or Minerva's lightning bolts fizzled out in the air and made all our hair stand on end, visions didn't always come when called, or they came in weird unhelpful flashes. But sometimes ...

Darkness, and the scent of smoke, like a candle had been blown out right in front of my face. I shivered, cold but also sweating. All around me, old stone walls reached up towards the sky, their broken tops lost in the darkness and the fog, empty stone windows looking out on nothingness.

Two indistinct shapes ahead of me in the darkness. One got up, swearing fearfully under his breath and ran away. The other sat over the extinguished candle and raised his hands – one empty, one holding a bulky Stanley knife.

Everything went dark before I could see him draw it across his palm.

Now I was climbing, my feet scrambling for purchase against the precarious black iron of the Holyrood Palace gates. Behind me there came yelling and flashing lights. I climbed, agony throbbing in my palm as it slipped on the iron, slick with blood.

I was at the top when my foot slipped out from under me. I fell, and an iron spike struck me right in the stomach ...

I gasped as the pain threw me out of the vision, and clasped my hands across my own stomach.

'What?' Minerva asked. 'Di? Did you ...'

'James,' I gasped. 'Lift your shirt.'

'Wha ...' James murmured. He still looked pale. In fact, he looked worse than pale. He blinked sluggishly and his head lolled sideways. I pushed his chair back and lifted up his shirt myself.

The fabric peeled back slowly, stickily. There was a puncture wound underneath his bottom rib, a steady stream of blood seeping down his jeans and pooling around his feet.

CHAPTER TWO

'Shit, no, *no*,' Vesta snarled through her teeth. 'You moron, Armstrong, why wouldn't you tell us?'

She dived for him, cloth in hand, kneeling in the blood that pooled around his feet to get a look. I stepped back, staring at James's face, his rolling eyes and slack jaw.

Why didn't we just take him to the emergency room?

If he died, *we* would have killed him ...

'James, look at me,' Minerva grabbed his head and turned it towards her, stroking and then slapping his cheeks, trying to get him to open his eyes. He groaned low in his throat. 'Damn it, Isobel, why did it have to be bridge night ... ?'

'All right, OK,' Vesta muttered, chucking the bloodied cloth into the sink and grabbing another. Her hands were shaking. 'Get me, I need ... I need bandages, lots of bandages, and the surgical gauze, and calendula and comfrey and lavender oil and the pestle and mortar.'

She pressed the cloth hard against the puncture wound in James's side, and he croaked out a thin cry of agony. I gasped with relief – if he was screaming, he was alive.

'Get the surgical stuff!' Minerva demanded, leaping from her chair and running out of the room.

I dived for the cupboard in the corner of the kitchen and fumbled over the combination lock. I didn't bother rummaging for armfuls of stuff; instead, I yanked out the whole basket full of gauze and bandages and deposited it by Vesta's elbow. She snatched up a packet of gauze, tore it open, her hands covered in James's blood, and pressed it to the wound.

Minerva ran back in, her hands full of bottles and packets, the big stone pestle and mortar balanced precariously in the crook of her elbow.

'Di, hold this on, hard,' Vesta said, and I knelt in the blood and took over pressing on James's stomach. Vesta leaped up and washed her hands in the sink, then grabbed the witchy ingredients and started throwing them into the mortar and grinding.

'Is that going to help?' I asked. Isobel had tried to teach me some of her remedies, but Vesta had a much better head for it. She didn't answer. That seemed like a bad sign. She gritted her teeth and twisted the pestle this way and that.

'Was he stabbed?' Minerva asked.

'He fell,' I said, redoubling the pressure. 'He was climbing the fence to get out of the abbey. Wrought iron spikes. His hand was bleeding. He slipped and fell.'

Minerva sucked her teeth in sympathy.

My other hand went back to my own stomach. 'I felt it,' I whispered.

Minerva winced.

'That's not all I saw. He was in the abbey, all right – sitting over a candle, holding a craft knife. He did that to his hand himself. It was like some kind of ritual.'

There was silence, apart from the grinding of Vesta's pestle and mortar and James's soft groaning, while this sank in.

'What do you reckon?' Minerva muttered. 'Was it ... *real*? Did you see anything, you know ... demonic?'

'No obvious demons,' I said. I looked up at James, but his eyes were shut – I didn't think he was in much of a state to answer our questions right now. 'We should ask him when he's properly awake. If he's done something stupid, we need to know.'

'OK, let me look,' Vesta said. I backed off, and she gently peeled away the gauze and then let out a sigh of relief that was music to my ears. 'It's a flesh wound, not too deep. You lucky bastard. A few millimetres deeper and you might've lost a kidney. Or died,' she added as an afterthought. 'Let's get him on to the sofa.'

She said it to both of us, but Minerva and I pretty much just hovered around her shoulders like anxious mayflies while Vesta gently hooked her arm under James's knees and lifted him off the chair. She carried him through to the sitting room and laid him down on the sofa, under the watchful eyes and claws of the taxidermy bear.

Minerva and I sank down on the chairs opposite,

and Vesta knelt by James's side and started applying the herbal mixture she'd made, muttering under her breath in clumsy Gaelic. I dug my fingers into the tangle of my hair and held my breath as James winced and I saw Vesta's shoulders tense – then they both relaxed, and James's head lolled back on the sofa cushions.

'We should have taken him to the hospital,' Minerva said.

'Shh!' Vesta stood up, gesturing for her sister to come away from the sofa. We both followed her out into the hall.

'We should call 911,' I agreed, slumping against the stairs and running my hands over the stiff feathers of the vulture. 'Who knows how much blood he's lost?'

'He said no,' Vesta shrugged. 'And the poultice is working. I say let him sleep it off.'

'What if he doesn't wake up?' Minerva said, biting her lip.

'Oh don't be dramatic, Min,' said Vesta. 'He's not going to die.'

'How do you know? How do you even know the poultice is working properly? All we know for sure is it knocked him out!'

'That's what it's supposed to do, it speeds up the healing! Isobel said ... '

'Hey!' I yelped, as a pale, shaky, bloodstained figure appeared in the doorway to the sitting room. Before I could grab him he streaked past like a fast-zombie, wrenched open the front door and staggered down the steps into the night. 'Hey, James, stop!'

'Yeah, I think the poultice definitely worked,' Vesta said, staring after him, nonplussed.

I followed him, taking the steps two at a time, gasping as the freezing, foggy air hit me in the face. James was a faint shadow slipping between the street lights, and then he was gone. I ran a few metres down the street and called his name into the deadening fog, but it was no good. I'd lost him.

I stood in the street for a moment, shivering, sending up a quick prayer to whatever powers watched over us that he would make it home – or to a hospital – before he fell down and froze to death. Then I turned to go back.

'Diana? Is that you?'

I twisted around at the words, half-expecting to see James before I realised the voice was more familiar than that. A shape emerged from the fog, but this one was sensibly wrapped up in a thick woollen overcoat, a few curls of hair springing out from underneath a tweedy flat cap.

'Sebastian,' I sighed. 'What are you doing here? It must be nearly one a.m.'

'Been out, you know, here and there,' Sebastian said, a little smugly. 'Isobel asked me to drop something in. Did you lose a teenage boy? Because I just nearly hit one with the car.'

'Oh lord,' I groaned, peering into the fog. 'Was he OK?'

'Well, he was bleeding, but I didn't get him. *This* close. He was running like he had a demon after him. Er – he didn't, did he?'

'... debatable. Come on, let's get inside.'

We traipsed up the steps and I shut and leaned on the door. Minerva and Vesta were still bickering in the hall, but their eyebrows rose as they saw Sebastian.

'Di, that's the wrong blond,' Vesta said. 'The one we were looking for was about this tall, pale, bloody?'

'I lost him,' I said. 'He ran off into the fog. Seb nearly hit him with Ruby.'

'See?' Minerva threw up her hands. 'If we'd taken him to A&E when we had the chance, we wouldn't have lost him. We could've asked him what kind of ritual he was trying to do!'

'Sorry, guys,' I said. 'I just missed him. We have his name, though. We'll just have to try Google and stalking.'

'Hm. Not necessarily!' said Sebastian. He paused to let this sink in, and then turned and went into the sitting room without explaining himself.

Minerva rolled her eyes at his dramatics, but Vesta shrugged and padded after him with an indulgent smile on her lips. As I entered the room, I saw him slip something out of his messenger bag and into a drawer – was that what he'd brought for Isobel? And would it be *so* bad to take a look as soon as he'd gone? – and then he leaned against the tall fireplace, resting an elbow on the mantelpiece. He looked like a TV detective about to reveal which of the guests at a country house was the murderer. In other words, really smug.

'So, what would you give for a little more information on this boy?'

'What information could you possibly have?' I said, playing along and frowning suspiciously at him.

Sebastian reached into his coat and pulled out something black, rectangular ...

'You stole his phone?' Minerva gasped.

'No,' said Sebastian, sagging a little. 'He dropped it when he was dodging Ruby's front bumper. But still, I picked it up, and now we have him! A little IT magic and your standard smartphone can be turned into a handy tracking device. Plus, you can have a poke around in his apps and read his private Facebook posts. So what did he do? Is he possessed?'

The three of us exchanged glances. 'Well ... we're not actually sure,' said Minerva, sinking down on to the sofa, carefully avoiding the small bloodstain that James had left. She ran her hands over her face. 'I was having such a good night. I'm sober now, and I don't like it.'

'We ran into him bleeding on the street,' I said. 'He broke into Holyrood Abbey and cut himself – this is vision intel, he didn't tell us that. I didn't *see* any demons. It could've just been, y'know ... really committed goths.'

'He didn't look like a goth,' said Vesta. 'And you said there were candles.'

'One candle,' I corrected. 'Anyway, we should definitely keep an eye on him, So go on, Q. Show us how this tracker stuff works.'

Sebastian was already shrugging off his bag and getting out his laptop. 'Just got to break into the phone. Lucky for us, he hasn't got half his security settings on right – could take a few minutes, though.' He rummaged in the bag, pulled out a handful of cables and found the right one to connect the phone to the laptop. 'Just got to download a couple of things ... OK, while that's running ...'

Vesta perched on the arm of the chair Sebastian was sitting in, one arm thrown over his shoulders and her feet swinging. I leaned against the wall and watched as his face flushed an adorable deep pink, starting at the tips of his ears. He fixed his eyes firmly on the screen.

I sat down beside Minerva and pulled out my phone.

Teasing him? on purpose? I typed into a chat window. Minerva shook her head and took the phone from me.

DOUBT IT. If she can't punch it or put a poultice on it, V doesn't give it much thought tbh.

I stifled a snigger at this spot-on description of Vesta, and looked back at the two of them – Sebastian panicking a little less, tipping his head back to say something to Vesta, Vesta draping herself over him for a better look at the screen. The guilelessness of it all made me grin.

'Got it,' said Sebastian. He swiped a couple of times over the phone's surface, and sure enough it lit up. 'Just installing the location tracker now.'

'Can I?' Minerva asked, reaching for the phone. Sebastian gestured for her to take it. She started tapping, swiping through screens. 'I see Facebook ... James Robert Armstrong, fifteen, single. Friends are mostly boys around his age ... not that many of them. Son of Julia Van Ness and ... oh. Remembering John Franklin Armstrong. His dad's dead.' She frowned. 'He doesn't post much – hasn't said anything about his dad, not even filtered or private. Maybe it happened a while ago. He's shared stuff about gaming, a couple of Lovecraft stories. Oh look, some casual homophobia, screw you Armstrong ... all seems pretty normal on the surface. He's a bit of a nerd.'

'Ha!' Vesta barked. 'Pot, meet kettle.'

'Did I say it was a bad thing?' Minerva shot back.

'Looks like he spends most of his time ... huh. That's the middle of nowhere,' Sebastian frowned. 'Hang on. Maps, maps ...'

I came around and leaned on the back of his chair so I could see. On the screen, a tangle of glowing green lines indicated all the places where the phone's location had been tracked. Seb seemed to be right – the biggest, most concentrated bunching together of lines was happening somewhere outside Edinburgh, up in the hills, in what seemed to be the middle of a field. Then Sebastian pulled up a clean map next to the tracker, and zoomed in.

'Aha! There's a school there. Oh, that's Wallington School.'

I whistled low under my breath. Even I had heard of Wallington. It was probably the poshest school in Scotland, a place where the Scottish upper classes sent their boys to be turned into tomorrow's politicians and bankers – and today's entitled hooligans, from what I'd heard. That seemed to give more weight to the 'teenagers mucking about' theory than the 'demonology' one, but we had to be sure.

'Boarding school explains why he spends so much time there,' Sebastian said. 'It looks like he's travelled into the city a lot too, and there's this loop out into the Pentland Hills . . . I wonder what he was doing out there?'

'Well, he's probably headed back to the school, if that's where he lives. I suggest we go ask him,' I said.

CHAPTER THREE

But first: home, sleep, and school.

Sadly, it had turned out that demon-hunting wasn't on the Scottish government's list of approved vocations, so the three of us were stuck doing our Highers like everybody else. Understanding the Scottish system in the first place, after moving from London, *after* moving from New York, had felt like one of those dreams I heard normal teenagers had about being given an exam they hadn't prepared for. I'd had to make notes.

I clattered down the stairs of the enormous Georgian townhouse where Dad and I were living, still doing up the buttons on my school shirt, Milly bouncing at my heels. Dad was in the kitchen as usual, eating toast with one hand and scrolling through a document on his laptop with the other. His study down in the basement was beautifully decorated these days: walls crammed with books on psychology and the occult, a deep red carpet, candles, instruments, computers. And yet, nine times out of ten, you'd find him at the table in the kitchen, with its clean, sweeping lines and sci-fi-looking appliances, in the middle of a chaotic pile of papers and bits of tech.

He looked up and grinned at me.

'Morning, sweetheart. Good time last night?'

I had to take a second to rewind past James Armstrong's flesh wound and the candle smoke in the dark and the rollercoaster drop in my stomach when I wondered if no, really, we should have taken him direct to hospital in the first place ...

'Oh yeah, the gig was amazing.' I grinned back. 'Glass Towers were incredible.'

'Not feeling too fragile?' Dad winked.

'Can't think what you're implying,' I said, plastering on my best innocent face. To be honest, I was feeling a little less than a hundred per cent, but it was down to the short sleep and the adrenaline comedown, not the beer.

Dad would be interested in James – I'd tell him later, though. There wasn't time for the full Jake Helsing: Paranormal Investigator treatment right now, and I knew that as soon as he heard there was a possible ritual involved he'd want to go through every little detail of what Armstrong had said and done.

I fished my Philosophy textbook out from underneath the pile of letters next to the juicer, and stuffed it into my bag. 'Is it *still* foggy out there?' I said, looking out through the window in the back door. I couldn't see more than about half a metre across the deck.

'I'm starting to get reports,' Dad said. 'People getting lost on their own streets, hurting themselves on things they can't see.'

I frowned. 'You think it could be occult?'

Dad stretched hugely, accidentally kicking Milly, who'd settled down on top of his foot under the table. 'Oh – sorry, pupper.' She gave him an offended look and rolled over. 'I'm not sure. How many days now?'

I tried to think when the last clear day had been. 'It rained on Monday, by Wednesday it was getting foggy. About three days?'

'Hmm. Too early to call, I think. Here.' Dad unearthed a plate with a couple of toasted English muffins on it from underneath a sheaf of papers and pushed it towards me. I grabbed the muffins, buttered them, smeared them with Nutella and had just bitten down when I heard a familiar *beep beep!* from outside.

'Uf. Gff gh,' I said.

'Have a good day!'

I waved the other muffin over my shoulder and took off for the front door, scooping up my bag and jacket on the way past.

Lights flashed in the fog at the bottom of the steps down from my front door. With the headlights to give me a hint, I could just about make out the small, blocky shape of Ruby, Sebastian's demon-hunting Mini Cooper. Vesta was in the passenger seat, so I slipped into the back next to Minerva, who was leaning her forehead against the window and wearing a pair of large sunglasses.

We crawled off around Royal Circus and out into the Friday morning traffic. Every car had its headlights on full blast, and the going was painfully slow. Sebastian sat hunched forward in the driver's seat, scanning for any hazards that might lunge suddenly out of the wall of fog. I stared out of the window at the weird way people and shops and other cars seemed to melt in and out of view, and tried not to imagine tentacles, or clawed hands, or swarms of moths ...

'Have you guys got sixth period off today, after History?' I said, partly to distract myself. 'We could head over to Wallington's then and see if we can find James.'

'Yep,' said Minerva and Vesta together.

Sebastian nodded. 'I've got Info Studies but I'll skip it,' he said. 'It won't be anything new.'

'Literally nothing in that class is new to you,' Vesta said. 'I don't know why you're even taking it.'

'Easy A,' Sebastian shrugged. 'And they don't do a Higher in hacking.'

We finally pulled into the small car park of Seventrees High School and piled out, heading off to registration and our first periods. I didn't envy Minerva her morning dose of Mandarin, but I wasn't exactly salivating to get to Philosophy either. I pretty much sleepwalked my way through the morning.

We all met for History in fifth period, sitting in a row along the back of the classroom. It was, along with Greek, one of the subjects that Isobel insisted all Demon Hunter kids traditionally studied – although I don't think that she really grasped how little use my coursework on the Swedish Empire in the seventeenth century was likely to be. When the class was finally let out, we all piled back into Ruby and headed off, out of the city, up into the Pentland Hills.

'Listen, I've been thinking about this,' Minerva said. She'd lost the sunglasses and twisted her hair up and pinned it at the back of her head – she was obviously feeling better. 'Wallington's a boys' school, plus James should remember the three of us, and he might make a run for it if he was really doing something demonic. I think Seb should go in alone for now.'

'So tell me why I'm ferrying you all up there too?' Sebastian asked.

'Hey, if you want to drop us off and face the possibly demonic boarding school all by your lonesome, fine by us,' said Vesta slyly.

'Well, we're nearly there now,' Sebastian said quickly.

The approach through the Pentland Hills to Wallington School for Boys was . . . well, it was shrouded in fog, so we all had to watch the GPS on Sebastian's phone in its cradle on Ruby's dashboard and just imagine the craggy slopes rising all around us, the dark lines of trees threading through the landscape, all that good stuff. Eventually we passed through a gate in a tall brick wall and trundled up a crunchy gravel drive between tall evergreen trees.

The school itself loomed, dark and Gothic-looking. On a nice sunny day, it probably looked like a welcoming, ivy-covered palace of education, but as Sebastian parked out front and all but the imposing frontage was lost in the fog I thought it was more like the decaying mansion from a thirties horror movie. One where everyone hung around in white nightdresses, slowly going mad . . .

I shook my head and tried to focus.

Get a grip, Diana. Tentacles in the fog? Nightdress-wearing scream queens? Demons might be real, but it's still 2016.

'OK. The tracking app's enabled, so unless this James is a lot smarter than he comes across on Facebook, when he picks up the phone we should be able to see where he goes and when. If I find him, what should I say?'

'Just try to get a read on him,' Minerva said.

'He's not going to come out and say, "Thanks for the phone. By the way I've summoned this demon . . ."' Vesta grinned. 'Just tell us if he does anything, y'know . . . *weird*.'

Sebastian shook his head as he unbuckled his seatbelt. 'Why do I get the feeling this is going to end with me getting stabbed or kidnapped or something?'

'God, so paranoid,' said Vesta, rolling her eyes melodramatically. 'When has anything like that ever happened to one of us? Obviously we would ride in on our white horses and *save* you, smart guy.'

'You promise?'

'*Always*,' said Vesta, leaning in close, an indulgent grin crossing her face.

Sebastian flushed, and clambered out of the car as if it was on fire. Behind Vesta's back, I gestured to Minerva – a small flail intended to convey *Are you kidding me? She really doesn't know she's doing this to him?*

Minerva made a *welp!* face and shook her head a little.

Sebastian disappeared into the dark front doorway of the school, and the three of us sat in the car until the cold seeped into our bones – which was pretty soon given that Ruby, as trusty as she was, was basically made out of tinfoil and string. No self-heating seats or insulated windows here. As soon as the engine turned off, our breath started to steam up the windows.

Minerva broke first. 'I'm away for a walk,' she huffed. 'Before my bum freezes to this seat.'

Vesta and I scrambled after her.

Minerva walked off along a gravel path that led between two perfectly green and well-kept patches of lawn. We followed her, and found ourselves circling a large war memorial, a bronze statue of a miserable-looking young man in a tin helmet and a baggy leather cape. As the fog lifted just a little, we could see as far as the wall we'd passed through into the school grounds. A thick hedge had been planted this side of it, hiding the bricks.

At first, I thought the place was deserted, which didn't help at all with the feeling that we were alone in a Gothic world that could turn on us at any moment. It seemed weird to me that we couldn't hear anything from the school – no sounds of chatter, of boys playing or yelling at each other, nothing. All I could hear was the faint caw of a crow, and ... a snipping sound. Like a giant pair of scissors. Sure enough, a figure appeared, moving along the hedge, using a pair of heavy metal shears to keep the bushes perfectly square.

God, Alex must be really playing on my mind these days, because yet again I seemed to be hallucinating that

42

it was him emerging from the fog. The shape of this man's head and the way his shoulders moved under the thick jacket with the words *Wallington Services* printed on the back reminded me of Alex, and so did the line of his jaw as he turned his head, and ...

And ...

'Di,' Vesta hissed. 'Do you see that?'

'Get behind me,' Minerva snarled, and stepped in front of me, raising her hand, tiny sparks starting to crackle between her fingers.

That was when I knew it really was him. I wasn't hallucinating. He was really there. Alex. The boy who ...

There was too much. Where do you start? With the sweet-natured guy who bought you cookies and coffee on the train, or the knee-tremblingly sexy guy who took you dancing and kissed you like you'd never been kissed before, or the dead-eyed monster who'd nearly killed you, your father and your friends on the orders of his demonic master?

Preferably not that last one.

I didn't know if *any* of those people were the real Alex. He'd had Kincaid in his head the whole time. He'd been ... *remade*. I didn't know exactly what that meant, and I didn't think I wanted to. Even if he was demon-free, maybe he wouldn't be the guy I thought he was. Maybe he wouldn't *want* to see the girl who'd broken his ribs and then brained him with a lump of quartz the size of his head. Maybe I'd just remind him of Kincaid ...

Maybe, maybe, maybe ... the urge to cut off all these dangling threads by simply marching over and saying 'hi' was almost irresistible. Maybe he'd see me and smile. Maybe he'd say he'd wanted to get in touch. Maybe . . .

But then I came back to my senses.

He hadn't seen us, even though lightning was crackling across Minerva's knuckles, and I didn't really want him to. Not like this. I put a hand on her shoulder and whispered, 'Min, no. Don't do anything.'

'Sure?' Vesta whispered back. 'Nobody would even see from the building if we wanted to go over and beat—'

'*I'm sure*,' I hissed. 'Let's just go back to the car.'

Minerva and Vesta exchanged glances, and I knew they were doing their twin-talk thing, having a whole discussion without needing to say a word. I had a horrible vision of the two of them deciding to run over there anyway, fists blazing. Then they shrugged and turned away in perfect unison.

'That can't be a coincidence, can it?' Minerva muttered, as they headed back to the car. 'Possible demon activity, and Puppet Boy turns up in the same place?'

I stopped at the war memorial, peering over the bronze statue's outstretched arm. Alex was just a grey smudge against the dark hedges now, but I watched him for a moment, snipping with his shears, putting them down, and then . . . he looked around. He looked right at me. My heart hammered against my ribs, but he didn't call out or move. He just looked in my direction, hesitated, and then looked away again. I must've been hidden by the fog.

Sebastian was waiting for us by Ruby, his arms crossed, hands tucked behind them.

'Any luck?' Minerva asked him. He went *hmmm*, and

got in the car. Once we were all inside and the engine was humming, he turned in his seat.

'Well, I didn't get to speak to James,' he said. 'The receptionist let slip he was here, though, so we know he made it back. He'll pick up his phone and we'll be able to track him. We can do some more research on the computer later, I cloned all his app profiles.'

I let out a sigh of relief. At least we hadn't killed him.

Sebastian pulled out of the car park and we trundled off back down the country roads, going slowly, high hedges rising on either side before falling away. For a while there was nothing between us and the steep, rolling fields but a low grey road barrier and the odd tree that whisked past through the fog.

'Seb? There was something else, wasn't there?' Vesta prompted, narrowing her eyes at him.

'Not ... exactly. Something about the whole place just felt ... *off.*'

'Off? How?' I asked, wishing I'd thought to go in there with him and try to take a reading.

'The receptionist really seemed to want to get rid of me, for a start,' said Seb, slowly. 'The phone was ringing the whole time. From the buttons, it looked like there were several lines ringing at once. She kept looking at her computer and typing while we were talking. And there were other desks in the office, but no other staff. I didn't see or hear another soul the whole time I was inside.' He shrugged, one hand on Ruby's steering wheel, the other picking at the sleeve of his cardigan. 'It doesn't sound like much when I say it out loud. It was just a weird feeling.'

'Your feelings are usually pretty accurate,' said Vesta, which made Sebastian perk up immediately.

'We'll keep an eye on the place, for sure,' said Minerva. She peered out through the windows. 'This is ridiculous. I know it's autumn, but it's so *gloomy* out there now, I can't see a thing.'

'We actually had a little weirdness of our own,' I began, figuring somehow it was my responsibility to tell him about Alex. 'We were—'

'Argh!' Sebastian yelped, and wrenched Ruby's steering wheel around, throwing the car into a hard left turn. I slammed hard against Minerva's shoulder and she gasped as her head struck the window. Vesta grabbed on to the dashboard so hard it bent under her fingers. The car wobbled to a halt with a crunching, sputtering kind of noise.

Sebastian thumped the dashboard.

'Bloody sheep!' he snapped.

Shakily I pulled myself upright and checked that Minerva was OK before peering out on to the darkened road. In the foggy twilight, I could see white shapes milling around on the road ahead of us. They were scattering pretty quickly into the fields to either side of the road. Although if I'd nearly been hit with a car, I would have scattered considerably faster.

'The fence must be broken,' Vesta muttered. 'No way they're meant to be on the road. I'm going to get out and drop-kick the stupid fuzzballs back into their field ...'

The Trinity piled out of the car and started shooing, while Sebastian sat in his seat and fiddled with the ignition. I did not like the pathetic coughing noises Ruby's engine was making.

Please don't let us be stuck out on the hills in the fog and the dark with only these sheep for company ...

'Come on, out of the way,' Minerva grumbled at the nearest sheep, waving her arms at it ineffectually.

I was starting to think Vesta might actually pick one up and punt it over the hedge, when I heard a sharp intake of breath and turned to find her staring down at something in the road. It was fluffy, but it wasn't really white any more. There were a few white and grey patches, but most of it was red.

The sheep's sides were trembling. It was still trying to breathe.

'Oh no,' Minerva put a hand across her mouth as she saw what we were looking at. 'Did we hit it with the car?'

I frowned, looked from the dying sheep to the car, and shook my head. 'Don't think so. Look how far away it is.'

'Also,' said Vesta, who'd knelt down by the sheep's head and was gingerly stroking between its ears, 'I don't think you can get a cut throat from being hit with a car.'

'What?' I peered in to look, and kind of wished I hadn't, as Vesta gently tipped the sheep's head back. Its throat was cut, all right – a long, clean slice right under its jaw. The muscles were exposed, the blood still gushing as the sheep struggled to hold on to life.

A dying sheep shouldn't make a Demon Hunter feel much of anything. But still, looking right at that wound made me shrink back. I wasn't sure why it chilled me like it did, until Minerva spoke up after a horrified pause.

'That's not an accident,' she said, her face pale in the reflected glow from Ruby's headlights. 'A person did this.'

'Why?' Vesta's face creased with fury. 'And they just left her here to die?'

I kind of wished she hadn't gendered the sheep. It made it worse, somehow.

'Let's move her out of the road,' I said. 'We can't drive over her, and other cars might come past here.'

Vesta scooped up the sheep, holding her head carefully, and placed her down in the grass on the other side of the broken fence. We stood and watched as the sheep's trembling slowed and stopped.

I made a decision. I fished out my phone, tipped the sheep's head back again with a muttered 'sorry', and took a photo.

'Ew,' said Sebastian, coming up behind us. 'Well that's morbid, Di.'

I pocketed the phone quickly, not wanting to look at the mess I'd captured right now.

'It's weird, is what it is. It could be vandals, or a serial killer in training, but I smell a ritual.'

'James?'

'Maybe. Or *someone* at the school. Maybe his friend who didn't follow through on Thursday night? Either way, I want to show Isobel.'

Sebastian sighed. 'Well, do you want the good news or the bad news?'

We all turned to look at him.

'The good news,' he said, 'is that there's a petrol station about a mile down the road.'

CHAPTER FOUR

The bad news of course, was that Ruby wasn't going anywhere unless she was pushed. Minerva and I made a token gesture towards helping push the car, but after a few minutes Vesta rolled her eyes and snapped, 'Useless. Get in the car and get warm, you pair of pansies.'

I could easily have questioned the logic of her belittling our strength – when compared to the average teenager I was damn strong, thanks very much, and the only reason our contribution was so insignificant was that she was literally blessed with magic super-strength – but instead, I got in the car.

Vesta put her back into it and we took off at a respectable speed down the winding track. The sun had set by now, not that we'd actually seen it for days. The only lights were Ruby's, and the dim reflection from the cat's eyes on the road.

As the gas station rolled into view, its brightly-lit forecourt like a beacon in the foggy darkness, we got out and pushed again, for the look of the thing. Then we left Sebastian to try to get Ruby un-stalled, and ducked into the blissfully warm shop. Vesta made a beeline for the coffee machine, and Minerva started poking around the travel sweets and the shelf of CDs with titles like *200 Best Carols Ever!* and *Firemen's Wives Sing Christmas!*. The shop was empty apart from us and the girl behind the counter, who was reading something on her phone and giggling. In the chilly darkness, barely able to see the road from the big plate glass windows, it could have been three a.m. instead of ... what was it, about five-thirty in the afternoon?

I grabbed myself a hot chocolate and then wandered over to where a suspended TV screen was playing the local news. A woman sat in front of a CG background of fog crawling across a map of Scotland. The sound was off, but she was subtitled in neon blue, with the slightly clumsy translation of all live subtitles:

central and eastern Scotland and the Midlands.
The public are adviced not to to make any
unnecessary journeys or drive too far from
their homes. A similar fog reported in
Paris has been causing accidents and severe
injuries. Meteorolologists
Meteorologists
are puzzled by the phenomenon as the two
weather systems seems unconnected and

I nudged Minerva.

'Are you seeing this? There's fog like this in Paris, too, and people getting hurt.'

'It is November,' said Minerva, cautiously. 'Season of mists . . .'

'Y'know, I'm starting to get tired of saying *It could be a coincidence*,' said Vesta, taking a sip of her coffee. 'We definitely need to take this to Isobel.'

We let ourselves into Isobel's house, and right away I knew something was off. For a start, all of the lights. There was also the way she didn't immediately confront us with the fact that we were late for training.

'I texted her, but she hasn't texted back,' Minerva said, then called, 'Isobel? *Isobel!*'

I fished my phone from my pocket and selected Isobel's picture, but the call went straight to voicemail – her phone must be turned off. That wasn't so unusual, I knew sometimes she forgot to charge it or just got tired of its 'incessant beeping'. The knowledge wasn't comforting.

The twins called Isobel's name up the stairs and down into the basement, but there was no answer. Vesta went through the passage behind the tapestry and into the secret stairwell that wound through the walls of the house, thinking Isobel might be in the private training dojo in the attic. But the sound of V yelling 'Isobel? Are you there?' reverberated unanswered around the house, like an unusually articulate ghost.

'I don't think she's been back since yesterday,' Minerva said, pointing to the sofa under the claws of the taxidermy

51

bear. 'Look – my note about the blood on the cushions is exactly where I left it. And so are the cushions! Isobel wouldn't leave her sofa with blood on it all day.'

'When did you last see her?' Sebastian asked.

Minerva hesitated, frowning. 'Wednesday evening, when we were training. We didn't see her at all yesterday.' She looked up at me, tears welling in the corners of her eyes. 'She wouldn't leave without telling us. Do you think something's . . . *happened* to her?'

Oriax.

I didn't say it aloud, but I guessed Minerva was thinking it too – the demon we had released from Kincaid's body was out there somewhere, and Isobel was a witch and a fighter, but she wasn't in a Trinity. She couldn't defeat a demon by herself.

There was another possibility, too. It prodded at my mind like a horrible little gremlin, but I didn't want to look at it, so I squeezed Minerva's hand and cast my gaze around the sitting room.

'Let's keep looking. Maybe she left a note or something and we just missed it,' I said, more cheerfully than I felt. I cast around the room, rubbing my palms together.

What would Isobel have touched, before she left? Perhaps I could use my power, get a reading, at least find out whether she had simply popped out for bridge club, or . . . something else. I laid my hand on the door handle, but I was getting nothing. Maybe the doorframe—

The swish of stiff fabric across the floor. I turned. The room was darker, less cluttered, and there was a smell of gas and smoke. Isobel sat down on the sofa and smiled at the man opposite her. I stared, amazed. It was one thing to know *Isobel was practically immortal. It was another to* see *her, barely any younger than she appeared in the present, wearing the hoop skirts and tough bodice of a Victorian lady. Her grey hair was piled up on top of her head in a complex system of buns, pinned with long, sharp-looking needles. Thick black lace encircled her neck and wrists.*

'Mr Jones,' she said. 'Thank you for paying me the courtesy of this visit. Tell me, your wife ... she gave birth on Friday morning, did she not? To a little girl?'

The vision swam before my eyes, and I reeled as I was cast back out into reality.

'Anything?' Minerva asked. I shook my head.

'Nothing about this.' I'd tell them all about it later. When we'd found Isobel alive and well.

The gremlin-thought chittered in the back of my head again.

What if we weren't going to find her alive?

Four hundred years ago, Isobel had sworn she would not leave this world until Kincaid was defeated, and in some weird twist of power and fate, the universe had listened to her.

But now, Kincaid was dead. We'd killed him months ago.

What if mortality had finally caught up with her? What if she had just ... *died*?

Vesta came back into the room, a little out of breath. 'I've looked everywhere, and everything seems normal,' she said, throwing up her arms. 'Maybe she's just gone out again? Maybe she forgot about training.'

We all turned to look at her.

'All right,' she conceded. 'No, it isn't that.'

I started running my palms over the walls and furniture, hoping to strike something useful. Mostly I got nothing, but there were a few flashes—

The house brand new and unfurnished, the air full of brick and sawdust . . .

Isobel alone, younger, her hair still blonde, unbound and hanging to the waist. She had a dead creature in her lap – a ferret, maybe? – and she stroked its fur gently as she worked on stitching . . .

The sound of gentle weeping. There was nobody in the room, but I could hear two women's voices, low and choked. Isobel walked in, dressed in a tough brown jacket and trousers – men's clothes, maybe Regency period. There were splashes of blood across her chest and all up her arms, her hair was wild around her face, and her shoulders shook as she let out a groan of grief and pain.

I pulled out of the vision, my head starting to throb. Isobel was all over this place. She'd lived here since it was built – the memories of this house and its contents were hers, and I was intruding, there was no doubt about it.

But I had to keep looking, at least a little longer.

I held out my hand, running it lightly over all the surfaces of the room, feeling a slight tug when I found something I could connect with. This one was a purple lava lamp . . .

'Kara, come back here this instant!'

I gasped as a girl with curly black hair a lot like mine ran past me and out of the room.

Mom?

I tried to turn and follow her into the hall, but I couldn't move – the vision wasn't following the girl, it was fixed on Isobel as she came into the sitting room and stopped by the fireplace, folding her arms. She was the most modern-looking I'd seen her, in a tartan skirt and grey cardigan. She looked furious.

'No, Isobel!' yelled a gut-wrenchingly familiar voice. 'I wanted to make it right with you, but I guess you can never understand.'

'If you leave tonight, don't ever bother coming back,' Isobel snarled.

The front door slammed.

I reeled and clutched at my head, feeling the blood pound against my fingertips through the skin on my temples. I took a step backwards and almost knocked a stuffed otter flying.

'Di?' said Minerva's voice, very far away. 'What, was it Isobel? Is she all right?'

... *Mom.* I swallowed and shook my head.

I knew that my mom had run away. I knew that she'd left her Trinity unbound, run from her destiny to live a peaceful life instead of fighting and dying. It'd meant that there was no Trinity in her generation. Kincaid would live another thirty years, and her Trinity sisters – the twins' mother, and Sebastian's – would be killed defending their home from demons they couldn't truly defeat.

I'd known that Isobel felt it was a betrayal. I guess I'd assumed they had argued.

Seeing it, even a tiny sliver of it, was a different thing.

'No, it wasn't her. I mean, it was her. It wasn't about

yesterday.' The vision had been focused on Isobel, on her anger and loss. I could still almost see her, clear in my imagination, standing in front of the mantelpiece surrounded by her animals, that look of pure fury on her face.

Had Isobel ever forgiven Kara? She seemed to trust *me*, and she treated me like one of the family ... but that wasn't the same thing.

She stood right there by the fireplace, and told her never to come home—

'Hold on. Hold it.' I froze, staring at the room in front of me.

Something was different. Something was ... *wrong*. I'd seen it, but I didn't know what it was.

'What? What did you see?' Minerva said, gingerly turning the lava lamp and looking at it, as if the answer was inside. But it wasn't. It was in something I was looking at right now, by the fireplace, where Isobel had stood in my vision ...

'There!' I pointed. 'See it?'

Minerva and Sebastian followed my pointing finger, then looked back at me blankly.

'Why is that fox staring at the wall?' I said. 'It normally faces out into the room, doesn't it? So why is it pointing the wrong way?'

Minerva hurried over to the taxidermy fox beside the fireplace. 'I can't see anything weird about it, it's just ... looking the wrong way.' She picked up the fox to turn it back to face the room, and something made a small *rrrrrrrr* noise on the wooden floor.

'Huh.' Vesta stepped forward and stopped it rolling

with her foot, then bent down and picked it up. 'I think it's a bullet.'

She held it out between her finger and thumb so we could all see. It wasn't bullet-shaped – at least, not like a modern design. It was a small sphere of metal, like shot from an old-fashioned rifle.

'Not like Isobel to leave ammo lying around,' said Vesta, peering down at the floor by the fox's paws. 'I don't see a bullet hole anywhere, though – I don't think it's been fired.'

She passed the bullet to Minerva, who rolled it between her fingers uneasily.

I bent down to put my hand on the fox's head and concentrated. It didn't come easily, but I could feel that there was something there. I could reach it if I shut my eyes, shut out the real world, ignored the throb of my blood in my temples . . .

Wrinkled hands pick up the fox and move it aside. They reach for the wood-panelled wall beside it. They push . . .

A stabbing pain in my forehead thrust me out of the vision, but I'd seen enough. I winced and clamped my hands to the sides of my head. 'Trick wall,' I managed. 'Something behind the panelling.'

'Sit down,' said Minerva quickly. 'No more visions for you. We'll handle this.'

I sank down on to the non-bloodied end of the sofa gratefully and tried to breathe through the thumping in my head as Vesta stepped forward and ran her hands over the wall beside the fireplace, tapping here and there. *Thud . . . thud . . . thud . . .*

Thock!

'Gotcha.' She grinned, and pushed the panel. It sank in a few millimetres, then popped out and swung aside smoothly.

'What's in there?' I asked, unable to see from the sofa, and unwilling to stand up until my eyeballs stopped pulsating.

'Weapons,' said Vesta, with awe in her voice. She turned to me, carefully holding up one of them – a black blade with a bone handle. 'I think this is obsidian. I think it's *really* old. There's a sickle in here too, like mine, only it's made of stone. A couple of little drawers ... more ammo, lead shot, black arrowheads, some really suspicious-looking green darts I don't wanna touch ... '

'Good call,' muttered Sebastian. 'This has to be one of those stashes Isobel said she didn't want to leave unattended while Kincaid was alive. I wouldn't be surprised if everything in here was magical.'

He looked slightly dismayed as Vesta pulled out the stone sickle, sniffed at it and gave it an appreciative twirl.

'But she did leave them,' Minerva frowned. 'Even with Kincaid gone, why would she open this cupboard and then vanish?'

'Wait – there is something missing.' Vesta turned around, holding an old wooden box. She tilted it so I could see inside. There was plush velvet lining around an empty slot in the shape of a long-barrelled pistol. 'She must've taken the pistol with her. And the ammo, too.'

'She went out armed,' said Minerva quietly. 'And not just with any weapon. An old, magical weapon. She was expecting a fight.'

There was an anxious pause.

'But we could have helped! Why didn't she tell us?' Vesta protested. 'Or at least leave a note? Why would she just *go*?'

'And why that weapon?' I wondered. 'Min, can I see the bullet?'

She handed it over, and as she did so, she frowned down at her fingers. 'There's definitely something odd about it,' she said. 'It's turned my skin kind of yellow.'

I rolled the bullet gingerly between my fingers. It did leave a very slight yellow smear behind. A little afraid of what I might smell, I put it close to my face and sniffed. The odour was strange – distinctive, but not exactly bad. It was sort of sweet, and sort of not. A bit like the smell of matches.

Minerva had been sniffing her fingers too. 'I think this might be ... *sulphur*,' she said.

'Like ... the stuff hell is supposed to smell of?' I asked, moving the bullet away from my face.

Minerva shrugged.

As we all contemplated this, Sebastian's laptop went *binglebingle* over in the corner of the room. He said 'Huh,' and went to lean over it with a frown creasing his forehead. 'That's ... that is ... *huh*.'

'Care to enlighten us, genius?' Vesta asked.

Sebastian took a deep breath and spun the laptop to face us. It was showing the map again, the one with the trace of where James's phone had been recently. 'I put an alert on the tracking software, so I'd know if – well, look.'

He tapped a couple of buttons, and a red line snaked

across the map. 'This is the last couple of hours. See, there's us driving up the road towards the school with the phone in the car. There's me giving in the phone at reception. It stops there for about ten minutes. Then it starts moving again ... and now watch.'

The line took off again, weaving a tiny pattern around what must be the corridors of the school – and then it left the building and headed out of the main gate, but instead of going down the road, it took a sharp turn, off the beaten track and through a field. It wavered erratically, as if James had been looking for something. It approached the road, crossed it, and paused for a few minutes – a clock was running in the top corner of the screen, ticking over at about three times real speed, and I saw 5:23 slip by ... 5:24, 5:25, 5:26 ... four minutes. Then the line was off, faster and straighter than before. James was running back towards the school.

'See it?' Sebastian asked.

I stared at the pattern on the screen, my head still aching a little. I felt like I had when staring at the fireplace, knowing I'd seen something, just not quite knowing *what*.

'He crossed the road at about twenty past five,' Minerva said slowly. 'We – we must have just missed him! That was just before we hit the sheep ... '

I remembered the poor dying animal's wound and felt sick. 'How long do you think it takes to catch a sheep and slit its throat?'

'Probably about four minutes. Why?' Vesta deadpanned.

'But he's gone back to the school,' Minerva said, throwing up her hands in defeat. 'How can we get in to

sulphurous bullets – and started walking. The last data point was somewhere in the park.

We piled into Ruby and set off at once. As we trundled through the streets of Edinburgh, past the fog-blurred strings of Christmas lights along the shopfronts, I stared at the floating, flashing silver stars on the lampposts and tried to logic my way out of the worst-case scenario.

Just because her phone stopped there, doesn't mean she did. Just because her phone is dead . . .

I'd only known Isobel a few months, but she was as much a part of Edinburgh for me as the castle – one day both might be gone, but it was impossible to imagine the city without them. I chewed my thumbnail and wondered how much stranger this must be for Vesta and Minerva. All their lives, Isobel had been in that house, not really aging or changing, just . . . waiting, training, watching.

What *would* you do, if you'd waited four hundred years for something to happen, and it finally did? She still had a Trinity to train and look after, but I suddenly doubted that the only change Isobel had wanted to make in her life was taking up bridge.

In any case, the data point in the park was all we had to go on. I had a creeping feeling that if we did find something, we would wish we hadn't.

As Sebastian turned Ruby on to the road past Holyrood Palace, I had a sudden attack of déjà-vu and threw Sebastian a broad smile. He threw me back a suspicious side-eye.

'What?'

'It's just that last time we drove up to this park together, you still hated me.'

Sebastian flushed. 'I didn't hate you.' He hesitated. 'I ... may have hated the *idea* of you, but that's not the same thing.'

I laughed at him, but then I remembered the look on Isobel's face again. Seb's mother had never forgiven mine for leaving. All those years, Rota had felt abandoned by Kara, betrayed by her.

Sebastian had forgiven me pretty quickly for my mother's decision, what with everything that went on with Kincaid that day. But then, he hadn't been born when it all happened.

Isobel had been there. Isobel remembered.

My own memories of Mom were of a woman who loved life, in all its forms, with a fierce gentleness. I'd felt so safe, with Mom on my side. Whether it was us against the steep side of a mountain, or a particularly tough math assignment, or the meanness of other kids, I knew she'd fight my corner, and never give in.

I remember the day I realised I couldn't return the favour. I couldn't fight in her corner – not against the cancer. I remember the way she looked at me. The things we didn't say.

She wasn't selfish. She wasn't a coward. I was gripped once more with a desperate need to be sure that Isobel knew it, that her memories of Kara Fleming weren't all stamping teenage feet and anger and grief ... When we found Isobel, I decided I was going to sit her down and make her talk to me about Mom. I would have to.

Then we parked in the lot at the bottom of the hill and got out into the chilly night air, and another memory hit me. Standing in this parking lot, around this car, picking up my phone and listening to my father choking as he tried to swallow back his pain to save me from Kincaid's trap. I shuddered and wrapped my scarf once more around my throat, and then I got out my phone and texted Dad.

> Isobel not at home for training. Something's up. We're out looking for her. Will call if not home in a couple of hours.

'So, the last data point is pretty close,' said Sebastian. 'But I don't think it's on the path. About five hundred metres in . . . ' he held his phone flat and slowly turned around, orienting himself by its compass. Then he pointed. ' . . . that direction.'

We stood in the beams of Ruby's headlights and looked out into the darkness.

'Maybe her phone just turned itself off,' Minerva said, hopefully. 'Maybe she dropped it and it broke.'

'Maybe,' I agreed. 'We still gotta look, though.'

'I know,' Minerva sighed. She zipped her jacket up to her throat and pulled her hat down over her ears. Sebastian buttoned his coat over his thick knitted sweater. Even Vesta was wearing gloves and a long-sleeved T-shirt instead of her habitual vest top tonight.

Walking into the fog in the darkness was like walking along the ocean floor. There was nothing outside the dim circles of our torches skimming the wet grass. The air swirled around us, off-black, faintly opaque. Trees and bushes swam into view and then past, like coral or the little statues you put in fishbowls.

We fanned out, walking in a line like the search parties you see on the news, making sure we could always see at least one of the others. I stumbled and swore as I stubbed my toe on a rock hidden in the shadows behind a patch of tall grass.

'Almost there,' Sebastian called out. 'We'd be able to see it, if we could see anything.' I couldn't make him out, but I saw his torch beam waving through the fog. 'Another twenty steps or so.'

'Isobel? Are you there?' Minerva's voice was cracked and quiet. There was no answer from the darkness.

Five more steps, ten, fifteen. I could hear a trio of rasping breaths, but as we walked, one of them grew heavier, shakier. To my right, the tall, dark shape that was Vesta slowed and stopped.

'God ... this air, I can't ... '

'Wait!' I called out to the other two. 'Stop. V, are you OK?'

'Bloody asthma,' Vesta gasped. 'The fog. It's too ... *cold*. Just need ... '

I shone my torch in her direction, in time to see her pull out her blue plastic inhaler from her coat pocket and fumble it in her thick gloves. It seemed to spring out of her hands. She made a grab for it, and only succeeded in sending it spinning into the darkness in front of us.

'*Goddamn stupid ...* ' Vesta croaked, and doubled over.

'Guys, huddle up, we've gotta find V's inhaler,' I called back to the others. I shone my light around so they'd find me, and when I could see them I turned and carefully picked my way to Vesta's side, then started shining my torch around at the grass at her feet. The others joined me, and we circled her slowly, searching, and ...

There was a plasticky *crunch*.

'Oh. I think I found it,' said Minerva meekly.

She handed the inhaler over, and Vesta brushed off the damp grass and raised it to her lips. There was a hiss. 'OK. Still works – *just*,' she said.

In the light from our torches, reflected up off the grass, I could dimly see their faces as we gathered around Vesta while she caught her breath.

'This is ridiculous,' Sebastian said. 'Even if there's anything here, we won't find it like this. I'd say we should come back in the morning, but the forecast said the fog wasn't going to get any better for at least three days.'

'We definitely don't have three days,' Minerva said, her voice unusually high – almost squeaky.

'I really wish you could punch fog,' grumbled Vesta, only wheezing very slightly.

I stared at her as a thought filtered slowly through from the back of my mind.

'Hey, try getting into the triangle. Remember when we did it accidentally, on the Mile, on the way back from the gig?'

'Not really,' said Minerva.

But Vesta nodded, plunging her hands and her inhaler

back into her pockets and taking a few careful steps backwards.

It took a moment, each of us trying to position ourselves so we could see each other and we had an even footing and there wasn't a bush in the way, but finally I felt it, something snapping into place, like when two magnets that have been sliding off each other suddenly turn the right way around. I felt the hair on my neck prickle and stand up, my curls seeming to tighten and pull at my scalp.

The invisible chains of power that linked the three of us wavered and crackled through the fog. I could actually *see* them, stirring the microscopic droplets of water in the air. I watched, breathing deeply as the grey air that was caught in the beam from Sebastian's torch started to rise. A thin rainbow rippled through the patch of light, and then the air was clearing, the fog boiling away. I could make out Vesta and Minerva: first the glowing purple marks on the insides of their wrists, and then their dim shapes in the darkness, and then ...

A hard blast of cold, wet air hit me in the face and I squeezed my eyes shut and threw up my hands to shield and brace myself. The wind chilled and chapped my fingers, and tossed my hair back.

Then it stopped. I lowered my arms and blinked my eyes open to see the scrubby grass and dripping trees all around us lit up with a silvery glow. For a moment, city girl that I was, I didn't know what was happening – then I looked up. The moon was full and the stars were bright. We were standing in the centre of a tunnel of clear air, while a few metres away the fog still roiled and swirled across the ground. This light was moonlight, clear and strong.

There was no sign of Isobel, but I could feel ... *something*, a tug on my heart almost like the pull to step into a triangle with the twins. I was scanning the ground for the glint of a cellphone screen, or for some sign of Isobel's presence – a tangle of silver hair, a dark splash of blood, even – when I saw it.

It hung in the air between us, a ... a *tear*, almost, like a rip in some invisible fabric. When I tilted my head I could see light leaking from it, different from the silver moonlight, soft and yellow.

I opened my mouth to point it out to the others, but before I could speak there was a sound like an oncoming train, a scream of wind and force, rising all around us. My hair whipped around in front of my face.

'V!' Sebastian gasped. I saw him drop his torch and lunge for Vesta.

Then I didn't see anything at all.

Sebastian's arms closed on nothing, and he tripped and landed on his knees. The wet grass soaked the fabric of his trousers.

She's gone.

He got up, brushed himself down. Shivered.

They've gone.

'Vesta!' he yelled, but his voice seemed to echo mockingly off the wall of fog all around him. 'Di! Minerva!'

Obviously, there was no reply.

Sebastian staggered across the bright, empty space towards where he thought the rip in the universe had been, but the light had vanished. And so had the Trinity.

He fumbled his mobile out of his pocket and called Vesta. Her phone was turned off. So was Minerva's. And Di's.

He stood in the dark, all alone, staring at the slowly encroaching fog with panic rising in his throat. Then the phone in his hand buzzed and let out a sound like a blaring car horn, so that he nearly fumbled it into the wet grass. He caught it and squinted down at the bright screen.

His mouth fell open.

'You are kidding me . . .'

I landed awkwardly on my hands and knees, jarring against a surface that was cold, hard and damp. I couldn't see a thing – even after I scraped the thorn-bush tangle of my hair out of my face, there was nothing in front of me except faint yellow light shining through yet more fog.

Disoriented, I ran my hand over the smooth, lumpy stones underneath me and stared into the darkness. *More* fog, already? Had it somehow learned our trick and come back stronger, like bacteria, or the Cybermen? I couldn't see either of the twins, even though we'd been standing barely two arm's lengths from each other.

'What was that?' I heard Minerva gasp.

'Min, you OK? V?' I called. 'Where am I? Did I black out?'

'Dunno, did *I*?' Vesta's voice answered back. 'Why am I standing on cobbles? Have you got cobbles?'

'What?' I looked down again at the rocks under my hand. They were regular and squarish, free from grass . . . 'Yes, I'm on cobblestones too!'

But if we weren't in Holyrood Park, then where the hell were we?

I got to my feet, wobbling a little. The ground felt unsteady, like I'd been on a playground carousel and had gone around a few times too many. I stared into the fog. Was that a dark shape in front of me? Was it one of the twins? I staggered towards it. I couldn't just stand there. I'd work out where we were, even if it meant walking into a wall, or off a cliff or . . .

Minerva screamed, a thin and breathy shriek that cut off with a gasp.

'Min?' Vesta shouted. 'Where are – oh my God!'

I twisted, slipping on the cobbles, and ran towards the voices. The faint light of a street lamp passed overhead. I couldn't see my friends. Where were they?

Something struck my left shoulder. After a sick moment of numb shock pain bloomed through it, and I shrieked and clutched at myself with a shaking hand that found a tear in my coat and came away slick and warm.

Blind, bleeding, gasping, I staggered back. What had hit me? I had no idea, I hadn't seen a thing. Backing away from where I thought the dark shape had come from, I looked wildly around, but I couldn't see it any more. Not even a black stain on the yellow-grey fog.

'Come on, you bastard!' I heard Vesta yell. 'Show

yourself!' She was somewhere to my right. But the strike had come from my left ...

I stopped moving, my breath hissing through my teeth, scanning the fog in front of me – and then, on pure reflex, before I knew why, I ducked. Something caught in my hair. I suppressed a shriek, remembering Oriax's evil moths flooding out of the wardrobe and tangling in my curls, and looked up. Where there should have been someone – a man, a demon, a swarm, *something* – I saw nothing.

No ... there was *fog*. I saw it move, dissipating as it tore free of my hair – the faintest hint of something like a claw made out of swirling mist.

'It's the fog!' I said through gritted teeth, staying low, my shoulder throbbing painfully as the fabric of my shirt dragged over the open wound.

'I know, I can't see a bloody thing!' Vesta growled.

'No, *it's the fog*! It got me too!'

There was something on the ground by my foot. I grabbed for it, not caring what it was as long as I could swing it with all my might, and found myself holding a splintered piece of wood, maybe a broken post, about as long and thick as my arm. I twisted, bringing the wood around in a vicious arc, splinters stabbing into the gloom. It didn't connect. I slashed again on the backswing, and again nothing.

I heard something go *clang*, and then came Minerva's voice, weak and breathless: 'Oh my God, the fog ...'

Bright and familiar bolts of lightning crackled through the mist somewhere to my left, and I hurried towards

72

them, whirling the splintered wood in a figure of eight ahead of me to ward off whatever was coming after us.

I found Minerva. She was grasping a metal roadworks sign like a shield, and when she lowered it, I saw she was holding her other arm tight to the side of her stomach, trembling with every painful breath.

Vesta twirled into sight, her hands raised, a long and slightly bent iron bar in each fist. 'How can we fight *fog*?' she snarled, and lashed out, a vicious one-two swipe at chest height that would have had any solid opponent on the ground clutching their broken ribs.

And then I saw it, lunging for her, out of the fog. A hand: four grasping fingers ending in long, cruel claws.

'On your left!' I yelled, pointing with my free hand, and then hissed as a red-hot flare of pain shot through my shoulder.

Vesta whirled around and the fingers closed on her iron bar instead of her neck. Just for a second they both held on, then the hand tugged, and Vesta lost her footing. She stumbled forwards into the murk and vanished. I heard her swear and grunt, but I couldn't see her.

'Have to clear the fog,' I gasped. 'Blast it away again!'

'I got it,' said Minerva. Lightning crackled between her fingers as she backed away. I held still, the piece of wood clutched in both hands, waiting for the snap – but it didn't come. Minerva must be off course, and now I couldn't see her ... we'd have to do this by feel. I forced myself not to move too fast. I shuffled, an eighth of a step at a time, trying to focus on the twins, trying to feel our connection.

The thing came up right in front of me, claws scything through the fog. I brought up my stick like a baseball bat . . .

Then an electric shiver ran up my spine, and I stood up straight. The stick dropped to my side. I didn't need it now.

The hand in front of my face twitched and vanished, and the fog began to roil and swirl – but this was different from how the fog in the park had gently boiled away. This time the grey mist seemed to be sucked *into* our net. It contracted, rolling like thunderclouds in reverse. Outside the triangle, our surroundings slowly started to become visible – a steep, cobbled alley between tall buildings. I glanced up and saw a black iron street lamp, and beyond that rows and rows of darkened windows, some with iron balconies, some with plants dripping down over their sills.

I still had absolutely no idea where we were.

I slowly raised my hand, the purple mark of the Demon Hunters blazing in the dim street. Vesta and Minerva did the same. I could feel them pulsing together, energy bouncing back and forth.

Beyond the alley, thin and ordinary fog cast halos around the street lights and the headlamps of cars passing by. But in between Minerva and Vesta and me, the fog was thick and grey, and it boiled and balled and squeezed down to the size of a truck, then a car, then a man . . .

I caught glimpses of red through the swirling mist. Red hands clawed the air. Something huge burst from the fog like a sail, leathery, dark . . . then another.

They were wings. *Huge* wings.

'Oh, what the ...'

There was a pained, angry, suppressed roar, and the demon shook itself free of the last of the fog.

Where Oriax had been black and smooth, made of moths and darkness, this thing was blood red and scaly. Like Oriax, it could have been called humanoid if you defined human as having a head, a torso, arms and legs. Both arms ended in four-fingered, clawed hands. Spines sprouted from the skin on the backs of its arms and across its shoulders.

It twitched and moaned, caught in our net of power, beating its enormous wings against the edges of the triangle. I felt them slap against the sides of its invisible cage, the taut threads of energy that connected me to the twins twanging like the bass string of a guitar.

The face was reptilian, pointed at the chin, with wide-set slits for a nose. There was no visible mouth – the groaning sound seemed to be coming from the demon's whole body, like old wood creaking in a high wind.

Its eyes were white from edge to edge. It turned them on me, and I found I couldn't look away. I heard a voice.

It was *my* voice.

I should step aside. I can't contain it. No mortal can.

I heard the words inside my head, but I knew they'd come from somewhere else. That wasn't me, those weren't my thoughts ... but those white eyes filled my world, and it was hard to remember what I'd been trying to ...

I felt the twanging cords of power weaken and fade. I looked down.

I had stepped aside and broken the triangle.

'Oh crap,' I muttered.

'V, watch out!' yelled Minerva. The demon lashed out with one enormous wing, tossing Vesta aside. She sprawled on the cobbles, then rolled unsteadily to her feet. The demon turned and advanced on her. I sprang towards it, but Minerva's lightning hit first, searing a black and smoking scar across the creature's back. It turned on Minerva and made a noise like iron girders dragging across each other – if metal could scream, it would sound like that.

She hit it again, and again, and I saw part of its chest peel away and dissipate into fog. Just like Oriax, it didn't bleed – it didn't seem to have organs or bones. It was simply . . . *matter.*

It screamed louder and beat its wings at Minerva, sharp, curved talons beating the air where her head had been with a clap like thunder – but she was ready for it, and she dropped and rolled to safety. I saw the thin trail of blood she left on the street, saw her try to get up, but then she gasped, curling around the wound in her side.

The demon turned on Vesta, and I saw my chance. I leaped, driving the splintered end of the wooden post into the creature's back with all my might, holding on, pushing down. The demon threw back its head in agony, and suddenly I could faintly see the cobbled street through the red skin of its back.

'No, you bastard, don't you dare—' I gasped, but it was too late. With one more beat of its enormous wings, it dissipated into fog and lifted off the ground. I fell right *through* it, landing on the road, throwing the wood aside at the last minute to avoid impaling myself on my own improvised stake. Rolling over, I stared up at the sky as the grey mist undulated like wings beating and then vanished into the dark sky.

'Oi!' Vesta yelled after it. 'Come back here and face me like a – like a *dragon!*'

But the fog was gone.

Oh God, I thought, not hurrying to get up from the nice, cool ground, my shoulder throbbing even more now that the adrenaline was fading. *We fought a dragon. And . . . we lost. I think.*

A moment later, Vesta was at Minerva's side, helping her up.

'I'm OK,' Minerva said, but her voice was thin and reedy. 'I think.'

'Keep the pressure on,' said Vesta, pulling off her gloves and slipping them under Minerva's side to soak up the blood.

I clambered to my feet too, hissing through my teeth as my shoulder shifted. Suddenly everything was pain. Everything that wasn't pain was cold, and everything that wasn't cold was hot . . . I wondered if you could get a fever from a cut this quickly, then kicked myself for thinking demonic injuries would work like ordinary ones.

I leaned against the nearest wall, by a door that looked markedly unofficial; definitely the back entrance to one of the buildings that loomed over us. There was a sign, some writing neatly embossed in white on a green plaque.

'Guys,' I said.

'We need to get you cleaned up,' said Vesta to her sister. 'I need to see your side.'

'You guys,' I said.

'Di's shoulder too,' Minerva insisted. 'We've got to get home. Where are we anyway?'

'*Guys.* I – I don't think we're in Kansas any more.'

They both frowned at me. I pointed to the sign.

'*Réservé aux employés. Pour livraisons, aller à la porte de la Rue Lamarck.*' Vesta read aloud slowly, in what sounded to me like a passable French accent. '*Défense de . . .*'

She broke off, looking around. A split second later I heard what she'd heard – running feet, coming closer. I spun around, wishing I hadn't dropped my splintered wooden post. I could see now that it must have broken off from a packing crate in a nearby doorway – and Vesta had wrenched her iron bars from a fence on the other side of the road.

The footsteps grew louder, and my pain-addled brain caught up with my fight-or-fight-some-more reflex. *Wait a minute. The demon has wings – it doesn't have three pairs of legs, and I'm pretty sure it wasn't wearing shoes . . .*

Sure enough, it wasn't a demon that rounded the corner at the end of the street and sprinted towards us – it was three girls. We stared at them, too confused to do anything else.

There was a tall, skinny white girl with wavy dark red hair in a gothic braided black coat; a short black girl wearing a jacket with an enormous fur-lined hood; and a curvy white girl with long golden-brown hair in a loose braid swinging down around her waist.

'*Ça va?*' said the girl with the long hair as she drew closer.

78

Yep. I think we're in France ...

I saw her register the blood on the street, and her eyes flicked from Minerva's wound to mine.

'*Oui, merci!*' Vesta called out. '*Nous ... nous sommes Anglaises, parlez-vous Anglais?*'

'It sounded like trouble,' gasped the black girl, dashing to Minerva's side. 'We heard. Do you need 'elp?'

Minerva, Vesta and I exchanged a look. I suddenly thought I knew a little how James Armstrong felt. We most certainly did need help – but if we rocked up to some French emergency room, with wounds we couldn't explain, and no way to say why we were even in the country ...

Could we trust these girls? There was no reason *not* to think so, but ...

'You also are bleeding,' said the tallest one, looking at my shoulder. 'It seems bad.' The thick, winged eyeliner crinkled at the sides of her eyes when she frowned. There was something about her face, her voice, it was ...

Oh. Wait. Are you ... my brain spun its wheels for a second like a truck stuck in mud as it tried to fit this person neatly into the *girl* or *boy* boxes it was so used to, and then I flushed guiltily, certain that whatever this stranger's gender identity was, I didn't need to be speculating about it right now, when we had more important things to worry about. Like my bleeding shoulder still sending throbbing waves of heat up the back of my neck.

She – *I mean, is it 'she'? Well, let's stick with 'she' for now* – might have caught me staring, because she raised a hand

and self-consciously tucked her hair behind her ears. It was a deep, unnatural, burgundy shade of red.

It complemented the purple tattoo on her wrist.

I looked again at her face, and then at the tattoo.

'Are you – a Demon Hunter?' I gasped.

CHAPTER SIX

I glanced at Vesta. 'V, what's the French for Demon Hunter?'

'*Chasseur de Démons*,' said the shortest French girl. She grabbed Vesta's hand and pulled it towards her, staring down at V's purple mark, mouth open.

'Oh, thank ... ' Minerva began, but then she stopped. Her eyes fluttered closed. 'Uh,' she said, and her knees buckled under her. Vesta and the short girl were both there to catch her before I could even blink.

'We will take you to Eva. She will know what to do,' said the curvy one. They helped Minerva to her feet, and she slung an arm over Vesta's shoulders.

'Is it far?' I asked.

'No, not far. That way.' The girl pointed, and Vesta steered Minerva down the street. She went slowly but steadily.

The streets were dim, lit by tall black iron street lights, and still wreathed in fog. It wasn't as thick as in Edinburgh, or as when the demon had been here, but we still couldn't see beyond the end of the road.

The other three Demon Hunters flanked us, watching carefully in case Minerva collapsed again.

'I am Francine,' said the girl with the long hair. 'This one is Coralie. This is Henri.'

Henri? Curiouser and curiouser, but if there was a time to mention my confusion, it was not right now.

'Diana,' I said, pointing to myself. 'Vesta. Minerva.'

'Why have you come to Paris?' said the short girl, Coralie, who was hurrying ahead and then hanging back as we walked, circling the group in a way that reminded me a little bit of a friendly sheepdog.

Oh, so we're in Paris? Good to know.

'Did you come to hunt the demon?' Coralie asked.

I exchanged a glance with Vesta. 'Well, no, not really – I actually don't know how we got here! We made a triangle and it just ... happened.'

'Oh.' Coralie threw me a confused look. 'Er – perhaps you 'ad better tell that to Eva!'

Paris seemed familiar and strange all at once. For me, big European cities always had a feeling in common; in London or Edinburgh or Prague, there was a sense that however new and shiny their buildings were, there was a heart underneath that had been beating for hundreds and hundreds of years. This part of Paris was winding and hilly, like the old town of Edinburgh, but somehow ... *neater.* More like it'd been designed, and less like a

82

thousand years of architecture had been scattered across the ground from a great height. Every sign seemed to be written in either twirling calligraphy or stiff art-nouveau capitals. Above us, more greenery draped from the upper balconies and a few lights were on behind the shuttered windows.

Francine led us up one of the hills, past darkened shops and cafés blazing with light and noise. There weren't as many Christmas decorations as there had been in Edinburgh, but I noticed strings of tinsel around some of the bar doors, and the bare branches of trees had been draped in strings of gold and silver lights. We passed one or two people on the street, but none of them seemed to notice the state Minerva was in – her breathing was heavy, but she soldiered on. Coralie seemed determined to distract her and Vesta from their situation – or maybe she just found it hard to stop talking.

'How long have you been in a Trinity?' she asked. 'We are very new – we bonded only this week! Did you three grow up together? Did you always know you were going to be Demon Hunters? You two are twins! Francine and me, we knew since we were babies we would be a Trinity, Eva told us, you'll like Eva, do you have a trainer? What family are they from?'

I let Vesta answer all the questions. I was less badly hurt than Minerva, but I was still feeling hot and sluggish. Perhaps it was just a lot warmer in Paris than Edinburgh – that made sense, since almost *everywhere* was warmer than Edinburgh. The heat spread over the back of my neck, prickling at me.

I decided to take off my coat. I wanted to have a better look at my injury, anyway. I slowed my walk, falling behind the others, as I carefully shrugged my right shoulder out of my coat and then gently pulled it off my left.

I hissed between my teeth at the sparking pain as the blood-matted fibres pulled away from the cut.

It was about the length of my hand, a ragged claw-mark, but not too deep.

It needed cleaning. There was fabric in it from my coat and shirt, and grit from the street.

I reached up with my right hand, and started to pick at the mess. Little stabs of pain ran through my shoulder as I touched the exposed nerves. I was still warm, but I could feel the cold air on the wound. It felt bad.

Good.

I stopped walking, let the sensation subside, tried to catch my breath. But before I knew what I was doing, my fingers had found the edge of the wound again. I couldn't help it. I needed to ...

I needed to feel the pain again.

I took hold of the torn skin around the claw-mark and peeled, gasping at the sensation.

The cold is good. The pain is good.

Deeper.

Heat burned the back of my neck. My breathing was short and heavy. Where were these thoughts coming from? Why did it all feel so ...

The hurt is good. The hurt is all I need.

If only I had a knife ...

I couldn't see. My vision was clouded with white, my fingers were working by themselves, digging in . . .

'Diana, stop this!'

A hand gripped my wrist, and I snapped back to reality. Henri was holding my arm, looking down at me, horror written over his – her – their face.

That moment of gender confusion actually helped: I came back to myself. My real befuddled, awkward, cold, tired self.

'Yow!' I yelped, glancing down at the bloody slice that the demon had taken out of my shoulder. 'God, that hurts! I . . . ' I looked at my hand, gripped by Henri's. The fingers were bloodied, right up to the knuckle. My gaze slowly travelled back to Henri's face, my hand starting to tremble. 'What the hell was I doing?'

Henri swallowed hard, and then tried to give me an encouraging smile.

'You will be all right,' they said. 'It is not far to Eva's house now.'

I lowered my arm, and Henri let me – but they stuck beside me as we climbed the last few metres of cobbled street to the top of the hill, and I was very glad they did.

The door where we stopped was much like all the rest – tall, thin and black, part of the same terrace that wound all the way up the hill. Coralie tapped a code into the entry system on the wall, the door buzzed and she pushed it open.

'Eva's apartment is at the top, and there is no elevator,' said Francine with an apologetic gesture towards the narrow stairs at the end of the short hallway. Minerva looked up and I saw her forehead crinkle as if she was holding back tears. Francine clearly saw it too. 'Cora, run up, get Eva and her friend.'

'It's OK,' said Vesta. She held her hands out to Minerva. 'C'mon, you've proved you're not dying, we're all very impressed, now hop on.'

Minerva weakly stuck her tongue out at her sister, then sank gratefully into her arms. Vesta lifted her like she weighed nothing and started up the stairs.

'Oooooh,' said Coralie. 'That is *fantastique*. I will run up and warn them you are coming!'

One moment she was there, and the next a small brown blur was streaking past Vesta, bouncing off the wall at the turn of the stairs and vanishing upwards. I stared after her, open-mouthed.

'Are you able to follow?' said Henri, turning to me.

I felt sick, shaky – it was actually *worse* now we were in from the cold and the dark – and my shoulder hurt and I didn't know what was happening to me.

But I *was* able to follow, so I nodded.

'Eva!' I heard Coralie shout from several floors up. 'We need you!'

I started up the stairs, quickly reaching Vesta and Minerva. Francine and Henri brought up the rear.

Eva's apartment was on the fourth floor, at the very top of the stairs. As we finally reached the landing, I looked up and saw a woman standing in the doorway. She was middle-aged, her hair in a sleek black bob with a fringe that came to a chic point like a swan's beak over her left

86

eye. She was wearing a black T-shirt tucked into black jeans, with a magenta silk scarf around her neck.

She stepped out on to the landing and held out her hands to help Minerva on to her feet, and I saw past her into the apartment.

There was another woman there. Elderly. Long grey hair in a braid.

'*Isobel!*' I cried. Vesta looked up, saw her great-aunt and nearly tripped up the last few steps. Minerva half-fell out of her arms and into Eva's with a yelp.

'What?' she gasped. 'Isobel, what are you doing here?'

Isobel looked puzzled. 'I came to help Eva, didn't – well don't stand there staring, girls, bring Minerva in. Quickly!'

We limped and staggered into Eva's apartment. Coralie was ready beside a black modernist-looking sofa with two sloshing bowls of clean water, towels and a first aid kit that nearly rivalled Isobel's. We sat Minerva down and she gingerly peeled off her coat and shirt to reveal a long tear across the side of her abdomen. Isobel and Eva knelt by her side, to start cleaning the wound and dressing it.

It was an eerie echo of our treatment of James, except competent and efficient. Perhaps that was unfair, but not *very* unfair.

'You'll need stitches,' said Isobel. 'But it's not deep or infected. Thank the Gods. You've been very lucky.'

'Ha! *Oh God ow*,' said Minerva.

'Isobel, why didn't you tell us where you were?' Vesta insisted. 'We were really worried!'

Isobel gave her a confused look. 'I did. Didn't you get my message?'

'No!' we all chorused.

'Where was it?' Vesta demanded. 'On the table?'

'Did you text us?' I suggested. 'Maybe it just bounced ...'

'No, I left a message on the answering machine,' Isobel said slowly, as if this was the most obvious thing in the world. 'The one on the landline, in the house.'

Minerva and Vesta looked at each other, and then chorused, '*What* landline?'

Vesta threw up her hands. 'You know nobody's used a landline answering machine for fifteen years? *Text us next time.*'

While we were staring at Isobel and she was staring back at us in equal confusion and annoyance, Eva patted the sofa beside Minerva.

'Diana, come, let us look at that shoulder,' she said.

I really wanted someone to look at my shoulder. It was throbbing. I thought it might be swelling up. But ... something made me hesitate. Something about what had happened on the way here ...

I didn't know how to tell them. I felt *ashamed*, and I didn't know why.

But once again, Henri had my back.

'There was a strange moment, as we were walking here,' they prompted.

Eva and Isobel looked at each other, and then looked at me.

'Diana – and Vesta too, all of you, this is important,'

88

Eva added, getting to her feet and looking around at us. 'How are you feeling? Any confusion? Strange thoughts you cannot quite control?' She looked directly at me, and her gaze strayed to the bloody mess on my shoulder. 'Any disturbing ... urges?'

'No,' said Vesta immediately. 'Why?'

I swallowed hard. 'I ... I ... yes,' I managed.

I could feel them all staring at me, like beams of prickling heat on my skin. What was happening to me? I wasn't the shy, shameful *type*. Other people's opinions could take a long walk off a short pier.

So why did my mouth suddenly feel like it was full of dry sand?

'Sit down, *ma chérie*,' said Eva kindly. 'It's OK. Tell me what happened.'

I sat, gingerly, and let Eva clean up my bloodied shoulder while Isobel numbed the flesh around Minerva's wound and began to stitch her skin together. Minerva leaned back, her breath hissing through her teeth, but she didn't relax into the sofa cushions – she kept her eyes on me.

I wanted to take a deep breath before I spoke again. But if I did, I thought that something deep inside me would break open. I really didn't want to cry.

'It happened on the way back here,' I forced myself to say. 'I found myself ... trying to ... to make it worse.' I held up my hand, and Vesta's eyes went wide as she saw the drying blood on my fingers. 'I was thinking ... stuff I didn't want to think ... '

A sob bubbled up in my throat and I clamped my mouth shut over it, refusing to let it out, to let it beat me.

'Diana, I promise you, everything will be all right,' said Eva. She covered my cut with a thick cotton pad and wound a bandage tightly around and under my armpit. 'Those were not your thoughts. You were being controlled by *le Dragon Rouge*.'

Even I had enough French to understand that.

The Red Dragon.

'Francine, go and put out the futons in the library,' Eva said. 'Don't worry, Diana. You will be all right now, and we don't have to talk any more about it tonight.'

'No, wait, there's something else,' I said, and the three French Demon Hunters stopped in the doorway and looked back at me. I swallowed. 'It started during the fight,' I went on, remembering, and breathing a little easier. 'I looked into its eyes, and it made me think I should move, break the triangle. I thought no, I wouldn't do it – but then I – I *did* it.'

Isobel sat down beside me. I braced myself. I knew I'd mucked up, but I wasn't sure I could take a stern talking-to, not with my shoulder throbbing and the sob still bunched up in my throat and these other girls watching . . .

But then she put her arms around me and gave me a long, warm hug. When she pulled away, she simply said, 'You three all need to rest. Go now. We will talk more in the morning.'

I must have got up off the sofa, been shown into Eva's library, taken off my dirty clothes and lain down on a futon, because that was how I woke up – stripped down to my underpants, with an aching back and a fuzzy head.

I struggled upright, groaning, joints popping. Weren't futons meant to be good for you? I felt like I'd slept on concrete. Give me a real mattress any day ...

A thin, greyish light was seeping in through the window. I shuddered as I blinked up at it and saw the ghostly outlines of the windows in the building opposite, wreathed with fog.

Paris. We're in Paris*!*

A long list of questions was starting to form in my head, now that there wasn't a dragon trying to claw my face off. *How the hell did we get to Paris?* was definitely up there with the most pressing ones.

It was daytime – Saturday, which was good, because I didn't think Seventrees High would accept 'we accidentally teleported to Paris' as an excuse for skipping class.

But whether it was morning or afternoon, I wasn't sure. The daylight was grey and soft, losing all sense of direction or intensity as it filtered through the fog. How long had we slept? When I fished in my jeans pocket for my phone and its clock, I found it was turned off; apparently out of battery.

The room we'd slept in was a library, but a very small one; it had probably been a bedroom when the apartment was built. The books were stacked two deep on floor-to-ceiling shelves all around the walls, and piled up on a desk by the window. When the two futons were unfurled, they covered the whole of the floor. Minerva was still asleep on the other one, her back to me, the stitched wound across her side rising and falling gently with her breath. She must've shared the futon with Vesta, but V was nowhere to be seen.

I got up and got dressed, careful not to disturb the bandage on my shoulder wound. It already felt much, much better. A benefit of being a Demon Hunter – since the bonding, my stamina had gone through the roof, and cuts and bruises seemed to heal a little faster too.

I was just starting to think of things like showers, coffee, maybe even food, when the door banged open. Vesta stood there, dripping wet, wearing only a towel.

'We have to call Sebastian!' she said. 'Where's your phone?'

Minerva sat bolt upright with a muttered 'Whasamada?', then winced and clutched her side. 'Ow. V ... '

'Seriously,' Vesta said, holding out her hand. 'Di, give me your phone, mine's bust!'

'What?' I said, feeling slow, blinking at Vesta. She tucked the towel tighter under her armpits and twisted her hair up into a wet golden bun.

'We left Sebastian alone in Holyrood Park, about twelve hours ago, in the dark!' Vesta said, as if explaining something to a small child. 'I was showering and it hit me: he has no idea where we are! God, he must be so worried. We have to call him, like right now!'

'Oh crap,' I muttered. 'My phone's out of battery. Min?'

Minerva gave Vesta a pained but shrewd grin. 'Thinking about Sebastian in the shower, were you?'

'Oh, shut up,' Vesta said, tossing her head dismissively, which made half of her hair cascade back out of the bun she'd just put it in. 'Don't think I won't kick your arse just because you're a bit banged up. Just hand over your phone.'

'Can't. It died when we arrived in Paris,' Minerva said.

'I got it out as soon as we materialised, or whatever, but it wouldn't turn on. Going through the … whatever it was … must have done something to it. And then, well, it kind of slipped my mind when I took a dragon claw to the stomach. We'll have to use Eva's. We should call Dad, too. He was expecting us back.'

'Oh God, and my dad,' I said, picking up a towel from a small pile that'd been left by the door. 'Shower first, then call Dad. *Le Dragon Rouge* … He is definitely going to want to hear about this.'

CHAPTER SEVEN

Sebastian put his feet up on Ruby's passenger seat, leaning against the driver's side door, his mobile sandwiched between his shoulder and his ear.

She's alive. They're all alive, and they're fine.

In fact, the longer he listened while Vesta went on about dragons and Minerva getting wounded and Di having some kind of psychological break – but she was OK now – the more he doubted that 'fine' completely covered it.

Still, Vesta talked and Sebastian listened. He slumped back against the seat and let her voice wash over him. She explained all about finding Isobel, a new Paris Trinity, a fog demon, while Sebastian's heart climbed down from his throat.

She's OK.

He would have let her go on for a long time, if it wasn't

for the small matter of the unconscious prep-school boy in the back of his car.

Sebastian swivelled in his seat.

James Armstrong was flat out in the back seat. He had blood smeared over his hands and mud splattered all the way up both legs and across the front of his white school shirt.

'Yeah, V,' he said. 'V? Vesta! Listen a second. Are you listening?'

'Of course I'm listening,' she said.

'After you vanished, I got an alert from the tracker on James's phone. I had it set to go off when he was within five hundred metres of me.'

He waited a few seconds as this sank in.

'Wait, what?' Vesta said.

There it is.

'Yeah. He was out in the park, too. I think he was heading for Holyrood Abbey again, or he'd just been there ...'

Sebastian sighed and took another nervous look out of the car windows at the tall gate of Wallington School.

'Never mind you three beaming yourselves to Paris – I could've done with some help right here. Do you know how to wake up someone who's been possessed and then dropped unconscious?' He frowned. 'He's breathing. I really think he's just fast asleep. But you know, is it like sleepwalkers, should I shake him or is he going to have a heart attack or something?'

'Slow down, Seb. What do you mean, "possessed"?'

'Well, I – OK, I'm not *sure* that's what happened.'

Sebastian reached over and gently prodded at Armstrong's shoulders. The boy made a snuffling noise, and Sebastian held his breath – but then he recognised the loud, crackling breathing sound. Armstrong was *snoring*.

'*You're on speakerphone now*,' said Vesta's voice, a little further away from the mic. '*Isobel's here*.'

'*Hello, Sebastian*,' said a familiar, elderly voice.

'*Hi Seb*,' said Minerva's voice.

'*Hey, sorry we left you behind!*' That was Diana's mongrel Californian-Londoner accent. '*How you doing?*'

'I'm – well, I'm fine *now*. I'd like to know just what you . . . ' Sebastian began.

'*C'mon Seb*,' Vesta interrupted. '*Armstrong, possession, right? One more time for the people at the back?*'

Sebastian pinched his nose and tried to rally. 'All right, so I was in Holyrood Park, and I got the alert that James was nearby, so I followed the GPS ping and I found him – just barely, he was wandering about in the fog without a torch or anything. If I hadn't been there I think he might've fallen down and frozen to death.'

'*What was he doing out there?*' Diana asked.

'Wouldn't say.' Sebastian looked back at Armstrong again and shook his head. 'I know you said he was tight-lipped when you guys found him before, but wow. Spies could take lessons from this kid. Anyway, I found him sitting on a rock, staring into space – not all there, if you ask me. His hands were covered in blood. I don't think it's all his.'

He heard a quartet of breaths on the other end of the line, sucked in slowly or hissed through teeth.

96

'When he saw me, he got up and ran off,' Sebastian went on. 'I suppose he thought he could lose me easily in the fog, but he didn't know I was tracking him, so it didn't do him much good – anyway when I caught up to him again he did this little panicky laugh and then fell over. He was a bit scratched up, but mostly fine. I helped him back to the car on a twisted ankle – I've got blood *all over* my cardigan – and I tried to get the truth out of him, but he clammed right up and then passed out. Maybe he was possessed, maybe he's just gone crazy . . . '

There was silence from the other end of the line. Sebastian frowned and glanced at the phone, worried he'd been cut off.

'Guys?'

'*We're here*,' said Minerva.

'So? What do I *do*?' Sebastian said. 'I can't sit out here much longer; someone's going to ask what I'm doing with one of their students unconscious and bloody in the back of my car! And I can't dump him back at school and hope for the best, can I? I mean, what if he's hurting *people*, not just sheep?'

'*If we were there*,' Vesta said darkly, '*I'd say bring him home and we'll make him talk. But we're . . . not.*'

'When are you coming home? Can't you just hop on the Eurostar?'

'*They could do better than that. But I need them here*,' said Isobel. Sebastian rolled his eyes and sagged down in his seat.

I need them too. I needed them first! he thought, knowing it sounded childish. *I haven't been trained for this. It's not like those Demon Hunter families where between Trinities all they have is boys and they just have to handle things – we've had Isobel, and the twins, and our mums before them. I'm meant to be back home behind a computer, Vesta's the one who deals with the bodies . . .*

'*Just . . . drop him off at school for now, we'll be back as soon as we can,*' said Diana.

'All right. Will do,' Sebastian sighed. 'Stay safe, guys.'

'*You too,*' said Vesta. There was a crackling sound, and he thought she'd hung up for a second before he heard her voice again, closer now. '*Hey, Seb,*' she said.

'Yeah?'

There was silence on the other end of the phone for a moment.

Is she . . . would she . . . is this . . .

Sebastian felt his face heat up, which was ridiculous. It wasn't as if she could see. The only person who might witness the embarrassing way he was biting his lip was currently unconscious . . .

'*You, um . . . I . . . oh my God get away from me, you nosy cow! Not you, Seb. Minerva and Diana are being awful because they think I can't see them, but* I can see you both*! You know what; I can't remember what I was going to say, I'll see you soon. Don't die without me.*'

'I – OK, I—'

But she was gone.

Sebastian stared at the phone in his hand for a minute.

What had she been going to say? What did she want to say that Minerva and Di couldn't be allowed to hear?

The heat in his cheeks was practically starting to steam up the windows of the car. He had to think about something else. Luckily, he had Armstrong.

There was only one thing for it – he was going to have to brazen this out: run into the school and tell them some half-truths about how he'd ended up with one of their students unconscious in his car.

I found him wandering on the roads, offered him a lift, and he passed out. That was at least a three-sevenths truth, if not a full half.

It was 8 a.m. on a Saturday, so hopefully the rest of the students would be having a lie-in, but there would definitely be teachers and staff up and about.

With one last glance back at the crumpled, snoring shape of Armstrong, Sebastian drove through the gates and up to the front entrance of the school. He thought about leaving behind his bloodstained cardigan, but it was just too damn cold, so he pulled it tight around his shoulders, hopped out of the car and tried the door.

It was locked. There was a bell, and he rang it, but after two, five, seven minutes had passed and still nobody had come, he folded his arms tight and turned away.

This wasn't right. It was just like the secretary's office when he'd left Armstrong's phone – an eerie air of silence, as if the whole building was holding its breath, waiting for him to leave.

Well, he wasn't going. James Armstrong was *their* problem, not his, and he wasn't leaving until he'd got rid of him. There had to be an out-of-hours office, or a back door, or *something*. Somebody in this place had to be awake and willing to deal with their wandering, potentially possessed students!

He started to walk around the building, but before he got very far he realised there was one other vehicle in the parking bay in front of the school. It was a small van, neatly painted in the Wallington School colours – Royal Blue and Better than You Gold – and labelled *Wallington Services*.

Sure enough, a little way across the grass behind the van, there was a figure in a blue-and-gold uniform just barely visible through the fog, raking the gravel path.

The phrase *rearranging the deckchairs on the Titanic* sprang to Sebastian's mind. Something was seriously off around here, but of course you couldn't have an imperfectly-raked path, even when the fog was so heavy you couldn't see it.

'Excuse me,' he called out to the figure, striding across the wet grass. 'I need some help. Do you know how I can get in?'

The figure turned and stared at him. The shape of its face was strangely familiar ... a square jaw, close-shaven hair ...

Sebastian froze.

Alexander. Kincaid's puppet.

A painful memory surfaced in Sebastian's mind. Almost *literally* painful – he thought he could feel the throb in his skull where he'd hit his head after Alex had thrown him down the stairs at the National Museum of Scotland. He could hear Di's panicked breathing as she fought to get out of Alex's grip, the sound fading as Sebastian was torn from consciousness ...

And then there were the twins. Alex had been the one holding them hostage. He was the one who'd given Minerva all those tiny scars under her chin and down her neck.

He'd made Vesta think he was going to murder her sister.

Sebastian clenched his fists.

He should knock this joker on his arse for hurting them – whether he was still under the demon's control or not – but a couple of things made him pause. Those things were Alex's muscles, bulging unnecessarily even in his shapeless maintenance uniform.

I'm built for speed, Sebastian thought. *I'm built for breaking and entering, not wrestling tall maniacs armed with rakes . . .*

'Um,' said Alexander, breaking the long silence. 'Sebastian, isn't it?'

'Is it you?' Sebastian snapped. 'Are you doing this?'

'Doing what? Are you here about the ritual?' Alex said.

'I – what? What ritual?' Sebastian said, before he could stop himself.

'The one the boys did the other night. I've been trying to keep an eye on it, but . . . ' he looked into the fog over Sebastian's shoulder. 'Where's Diana? Is she OK?'

'It's none of your business how Di is,' Sebastian frowned. This was not going exactly how he'd anticipated.

'Are they here? The Trinity? I wanted to get in touch, to tell them what happened, but, I . . . I don't know, I thought if it came from me they'd think . . . '

'They're not here,' Sebastian said through gritted teeth. 'They're ... busy.'

Alex turned his rake in his hands, almost nervously. 'Oh. I mean, no offence, mate, but I'd rather talk to them.'

'I bet you would!' Sebastian let out an angry laugh. 'So you can trick your way back into Di's good books and then turn her in to your moth-demon pal?'

Alex flinched. He twisted his hands around the wooden handle of the rake, as if he could wring it out like a towel. When he spoke again, his voice was low and quiet, as if he was talking to himself. 'If you knew what it was like ... being ... *remade* ... If you knew, you wouldn't say that to me.'

There was an awkward pause. Sebastian stared at Alexander, and he stared back. Then Alex stabbed the rake into the grass handle-first like a warrior planting his spear.

'Diana saved my life in more ways than one,' he said. 'She saw I needed her help. She believed that I was *still in here*. I'm free now and I'm never going back. Do you believe me?'

Sebastian looked him over. 'I don't know,' he answered honestly. 'But if you want to prove it, you can start by helping me with something.'

It was certainly easier to carry the unconscious Armstrong between the two of them. Sebastian didn't feel remotely bad about letting Alexander take the boy's arms, and most of his weight. He did feel faintly absurd, though, sneaking a bloodied non-corpse in through the staff entrance to the enormous brown stone building.

Slapstick comedies had been made out of less, but absolutely nothing about this was funny.

'Are you sure?' Sebastian asked, for the second time, shifting his grip on the boy's legs. 'Dump him in the doctor's office, that's your plan? Won't anyone ask where he came from?'

'You'd think so, wouldn't you?' Alex said darkly, shaking his head. 'You'll see.'

If this is a trap, how quickly can I get off a call to the police? I don't have a free hand to go for my phone, Sebastian thought. *I'll have to drop Armstrong and leg it for the gate . . . I wonder if it's remote-locking . . . I wonder who has the controls . . .*

'When I applied for this job I thought it would be nice and quiet,' Alex went on, apparently oblivious to the worst-case scenarios charging through Sebastian's mind. '*Gardening*. How much excitement could there be, right?'

Is he trying to be . . . chummy? Sebastian wondered. Well, it wasn't going to work. *For all I know, you're leading us right into the demon's lair.*

And the only reason I'm going along with it is because I'd rather have Armstrong in a demon's lair than in my car . . .

It wasn't a very Demon Hunter thought. Sebastian shifted his grip on Armstrong's ankles again, feeling guilty.

'You said, "You'll see". *What* will I see?' he demanded, as they rounded the corner of the building.

'Hard to say.'

Sebastian was just winding up to another sarcastic comment when Alex went on, his voice hollow. 'A week ago I saw a boy throw a fit in the middle of the lawn.

He was scratching at himself and crying. I've seen more than one of them with bandages on their arms. One of them fainted. I honestly thought it was all just ... posh boy cabin fever, you know? The kind of hysteria you get when you pack a couple of hundred entitled teenagers into a dormitory and then tell them they've got exams in two weeks' time.'

Sebastian suppressed a snigger. 'Are you sure it isn't just that?'

'The bottle of blood was the first thing that made me think not,' said Alex flatly.

' ... are you *trying* to creep me out?' Sebastian muttered.

'Don't be ridiculous,' said Alex, in a sweet tone of voice that definitely meant *yes*.

They reached a door with a neat blue sign that said STAFF ONLY.

'I found it hidden in the gardens,' Alex said. 'Hold on to him a minute while I get the door open.' A moment of awkward manoeuvring later, Sebastian had Armstrong's limp arms draped around his neck while Alex fumbled in a pocket for his key-card.

'You found a bottle of blood,' Sebastian deadpanned. '*You* just *happened* to stumble across a bottle ... *of blood*.'

'A plastic bottle. The label was ripped off but I reckon it used to be Highland Spring.'

Sebastian glared at him.

'Believe me, I wanted it to be nothing,' Alex added, lowering his voice as he took Armstrong's shoulders and led the way through the door and along a wood-panelled corridor hung with portraits of old white men wearing black academic gowns. 'The real trouble started when I showed it to the Deputy Head.'

There was still no noise but their footsteps, as they made their way past gleaming trophy cabinets and into a white-walled hallway. Sebastian fought the urge to hold his breath and try to make himself small, as if he could get through this without attracting the attention of ... *something*, if only he was careful enough.

'They started closing ranks, cancelling lessons. They've gone down to a skeleton staff. I'm pretty sure they only kept me on because I already knew there was something strange happening and they didn't want me going to the papers.'

'But that's mad,' Sebastian hissed. 'What about the students? Are they holding them hostage or what? What about their parents?'

'You see?' Alex muttered back. 'This is why I need Diana! The Trinity, I mean. Something's really wrong in this school, and I can't find out what by myself.'

He backed through a swinging white door, and into a large room lined with beds and smelling very strongly of disinfectant. Sebastian tried not to let his jaw drop. *This* was their doctor's office? In his school, the nurse's office was literally inside a cupboard, surrounded by miscellaneous paperwork and an old broken drum kit. Wallington had its own real hospital ward, right down to the zombie-green paint on the walls and the middle-aged woman in dark blue scrubs who was hurrying down the room towards them.

'Alexander, what's happened now?' she demanded. She

gave Sebastian a look of deep suspicion and annoyance, before her gaze fell on Armstrong's pale face, and her demeanour changed. She straightened up. 'Bed three,' she told Alex, who dutifully laid Armstrong down on the bed. 'Thank you. You can go.'

'Hey,' Sebastian began. 'Don't you want to know about—'

'Thank you for your concern, young man. It was very kind of you to bring the boy back to us. I can take it from here,' said the doctor. She glanced again at Alex. 'You. Can. Go.'

Received loud and clear, Sebastian thought, staring around at the impeccably clean ward and the huddled shapes of boys in two of the beds. *You can go, or else . . .*

'Yes, doctor,' said Alex, and his hand clamped down on Sebastian's shoulder. Sebastian tried to shake him off, but Alex squeezed. 'Come on, *sir*, I'll show you the way out.'

'So, like, should we talk about the fact that one of them's a boy?' Vesta said under her breath.

We were in Eva's kitchen, just the three of us eating toast and using Eva's phone to call our parents, while Eva and Isobel sorted out some things in the living room. The other Trinity were on their way over.

'V,' said Minerva.

Vesta shrugged with both arms. 'What?'

'She sort-of has a point,' I said gingerly. 'I'm new to this, but Demon Hunters are girls, right? I mean . . . born girls? I thought?'

Minerva blinked and took a deep breath, and I

immediately felt bad. I'd seen her gather herself like that a couple of times at school. That was her *gimme a second while I put on my Spokesperson for All Gays Hat* expression. She'd never had to use it on me before.

'They're a Trinity, right? They bonded, right? Henri's got the symbol, they've got powers like the rest of us, presumably?'

Vesta and I both nodded.

'Well, that seems a lot more evidence that they're not a boy than whatever they might've been called at birth, doesn't it?'

More nods. Slightly more hesitant, but definitely nods.

'Anyway,' said Minerva, 'he – *dammit* – she doesn't seem like she *wants* to be seen as a boy.'

'But this is incredible!' Vesta said, her scepticism starting to melt into excitement. 'This has never happened before!'

'That we know of,' I said thoughtfully. 'But it makes sense if you think about it, doesn't it? Like, lots of trans people feel like they were born in the wrong body . . . ?' I tried to stop myself from casting a glance at Minerva for her Official LGBT Stamp of Approval on this statement. I failed. She made a *well it's more complicated than that face*, but she didn't interrupt me. 'I guess whatever it is that gives us our powers . . . agrees with them.'

We lapsed into silence, munching on our slices of toast. I wasn't sure if the others were considering the metaphysical and theological ramifications of that thought, but the slow smile that crossed Minerva's face made me think she might be.

'Oh no,' I heard Eva say suddenly. 'Another? *Mon dieu. Tout est de ma faute . . .*'

'No, it's not,' said Isobel sternly. 'Do you hear me, Eva? It is the demon's fault, not yours.'

I glanced at the others, then stood up and went into the living room, my coffee cup clutched in both hands.

'What's the matter?' I said. Isobel and Eva both turned to look at me, then Eva shook her head sadly and gestured to the TV screen in the corner of the room.

The news was on. It was in French, and I couldn't hope to keep up with what the presenter was saying, but there were shots of major Paris landmarks – the Eiffel Tower, Notre Dame – all deserted, police patrolling restlessly. Then the screen filled with flowers. It pulled out to show one of the bridges over the Seine. The fog was much too thick to see to the other side, but all along the railing there were bunches of flowers, ribbons and candles, cardboard hearts going soggy in the damp air.

My mouth had gone dry. I swallowed stiffly and thought of the blank white of *le Dragon Rouge*'s eyes, filling my world.

The desire to hurt, to dig deeper, was gone now. But the memory of it made me feel like I was going to throw up.

'You see why I had to come,' said Isobel quietly.

'I don't – what *happened*?' Minerva said, coming into the room behind me. 'Did the demon kill a bunch of people?'

'Yes and no,' muttered Eva.

There was a high-speed rap on the door, and Eva opened it to let Coralie in. Eventually Francine and Henri came in behind her.

'Allo!' said Coralie, giving us all a friendly smile. 'So, we are killing a demon today?'

'Cora,' said Henri, and gestured to the screen.

'Oh *merde*,' said Francine. '*Un autre?*'

'*Plus d'un*,' said Eva, shaking her head and turning away, leaning with both hands on the table by the window. There was a map laid out on it, and a radio receiver. She switched it on, and I heard a crackly voice begin to speak, and others respond. I didn't need to know the French to guess it was probably a police radio channel. Her shoulders hunched and tense, she reached out and stabbed a red pin into an area of the map that was already a cluster of red.

'What's happening, Isobel?' Vesta asked. 'In English?'

'*Le Dragon Rouge* is killing people,' said Isobel. 'But it doesn't draw its power from battle. It doesn't murder its victims with its own hands – not unless it feels threatened.'

'Then what does it do?' asked Vesta, but Isobel and Minerva were both looking at me.

'Diana?' Isobel prompted.

I swallowed again. *Thanks, Isobel*, I thought. Did this really have to be an interactive lesson?

I forced the words out, as smoothly as I could. 'It makes them hurt themselves. It's making people kill themselves.'

Isobel gave me a small, proud nod. 'Good. Always name your fears, Diana. Its demonic hold on you has faded. Now you mustn't let the experience stop you facing it with clear, open eyes.'

I nodded, suddenly struggling against a head full of feelings, pressing my lips together so they wouldn't tremble.

109

'Wait,' said Vesta. 'Weird fog? People acting crazy, hurting themselves? Sound familiar to either of you two?'

Minerva frowned. 'You think James is possessed by the Dragon?'

'Is this the boy Sebastian found last night?' Isobel asked.

'We found him on the street on Thursday night, after the concert,' said Minerva. 'He'd cut himself – Di saw it in a vision. Doing some kind of ritual in Holyrood Abbey. He's been behaving weirdly ever since. Diana, show her the sheep.'

Reluctantly, I fished my now-recharged cellphone from my pocket and pulled up the photograph of the poor sheep's cut throat. Isobel looked at it, her lip twisting with a disgust that I suspected was more to do with the act of violence than the gory image.

'You should have told me about this,' she said.

'Could've done, if you'd texted us like a normal person,' Vesta murmured. Isobel shot her a stern look and she dipped her head apologetically.

'That can't be right.' Eva had turned around, leaning on the map table, her arms folded. 'The demon cannot be in two places at once.'

But she didn't sound completely certain.

'Unless, when we opened the portal, to bring me here . . . ' Isobel said slowly.

Eva's face fell. '*Oh mon dieu—*'

'It's not this bad in Edinburgh though,' I said quickly. 'Perhaps it's got through, but it's still concentrating on Paris? We haven't had any of this . . . ' I gestured to the

TV screen, and then gulped as I understood what it was showing me now. The screen was filled with photographs – selfies, family holidays, professional headshots ...

Ten people? Twenty, or more?

The victims of the Dragon.

I tried not to think about their families. I tried not to think about the people of Paris, wondering what on earth was going on in their city ...

'People must be terrified,' murmured Minerva. 'They must think they're in the middle of an epidemic ...'

'They *are* afraid,' said Francine. 'My parents know it is a demon, so they do not want me to leave the house by myself.'

'My mother has gone home to Pralognan,' said Henri. 'It is high in the Alps, she will be safe there, and I stay with Coralie. We will all be safer.' There was determination in the set of Henri's plum-coloured lips, but you couldn't miss the waver in their voice.

'So how do we kill it?' Vesta asked, hands on her hips. 'It's not possessing anyone, so we ought to be able to kill it, right?'

'But Di stabbed it right through with a wooden stake and it just melted back into fog,' Minerva pointed out.

'That is where Isobel comes in,' said Eva.

Isobel reached into the pocket of her cardigan, and drew out a gun. I saw Minerva take a wary half-step backwards. 'This was made for me by a gunsmith in 1820. It fires bullets made with lead and sulphur.'

Minerva, Vesta and I exchanged glances. So it *was* sulphur ...

111

'When the Dragon has taken form, penetrating it with sulphur should weaken it enough that it can't become fog again. Then you can kill it, as you would kill any other demon. Cut off its head.'

I nodded, remembering with a shiver the brutal night she had made us spend in the local butchery warehouse, chopping the heads off pig carcasses. *It will be easier than this*, she'd told us. *No demon has blood or sinews like this. But you need to know what it's like to look into something's eyes and still make that cut.*

'With Eva and I here, and one Trinity to hold the demon, it was doable,' said Isobel. 'But I must say I'm glad you girls have come. With two full Trinities . . .' she hesitated. I guessed she still didn't want to imply it'd be a piece of cake.

'We are going to kill it very, very dead,' said Coralie.

Isobel simply smiled. Eva nodded, though she looked a little bit green.

'We 'ave been mapping the locations of the deaths, to see if there's a pattern,' said Henri, going over to the map. I followed and looked down at the red pins. They were scattered all over the city, apart from one cluster that was so tightly packed with pins it was hard to see what location was underneath.

'That is the Pont d'Iéna. It's the bridge right next to the Eiffel Tower,' Francine said. 'That's where we'll have the best chance of catching and killing the Dragon.'

'Well, two Trinities are all very well,' said Vesta, 'but we didn't bring our weapons with us. We were fighting it off with sticks before, and Minerva was almost

112

disembowelled! We're going to need to tool up before we face it again.'

Eva smiled, for the first time this morning.

'Do not worry, *ma chérie*,' she said. 'With this, I can help you.'

CHAPTER EIGHT

'We have a proud history here,' said Eva, as she fished the key out of her pocket. We had followed her down the stairs from her apartment, thinking that she would take us to a lock-up or a storage facility or some kind of secret lair in the sewers, but in fact we had only gone as far as the basement.

It looked like an ordinary basement in any apartment building. Two bicycles leaned against the walls. A few metal shelves on the other side were full of plastic boxes, nails and tins of wood polish. There was a musty, not-unpleasant smell of turpentine and wood shavings and damp.

At least, that was all I saw when I first walked into the small room. But Minerva nudged me and pointed, and when I looked I saw the black glint of a CCTV camera, half-obscured behind a collection of old glue bottles.

'France has one of the longest unbroken Demon Hunter lines in the world,' said Eva, with pride. 'My own foremother was *Parisii* before the Roman Empire – at least, family legend says so. We have been here through riot and revolution and occupation. Consistency has allowed us to put down deep roots. Demon Hunters planned this building.'

She lifted an old rug from the floor – it was faded and grey, but seemed much heavier than it looked. Vesta bent down and helped her move it aside to reveal a rusty trapdoor. Eva knelt and unlocked it – it looked like it ought to make a shrieking noise as it opened, but it swung smoothly aside. Underneath there was a flight of clean, solid-looking wooden stairs.

'After you,' Eva said to Isobel, stepping aside. Isobel nodded to her graciously and descended the stairs. When she was about halfway down, a light went on – it must have been a motion sensor – and I saw the glint of metal.

The Paris armoury was like the Batcave, if Bruce Wayne had got rid of all the bats and stalagmites and filled the space with weapons instead. They were hung from the ceiling, stacked on shelves, locked away in cabinets. Swords and knives and axes, longbows and crossbows and shotguns, helmets and chainmail and Kevlar vests. There was even a workbench area that looked like it'd been used for repairs for several hundred years. A tall cabinet beside it had a hundred different small drawers, each one neatly labelled. Probably full of witchy ingredients and crafting gear, just like Isobel's cupboard back in Edinburgh.

Vesta and Minerva were looking around in wonder

too, and Vesta turned full-circle two or three times before looking at Eva with a gleeful, hopeful smile on her face.

'Help yourselves,' said Eva. 'Just remember that there are a lot of police on the streets today, and we will be right in the centre of Paris. No spears or morning stars, please! This will have to be a little more covert than that.'

'Thank you,' said Minerva, as Vesta immediately ran over to a display of hunting knives. 'This is amazing.'

'Here, let me find you a vest to cover your injury,' Eva said.

I wandered among the weapons, uncertain what I ought to pick. I missed my *naginata*, but spears were out of the question, and I guessed the same went for anything longer than I was.

I saw Isobel looking appreciatively at a rack of gleaming rapiers with ornate, twirling metal handles. Minerva had gone straight for the crossbows – her personal weapon at home was a collapsible, modern black steel hunting crossbow, but she picked up a heavy antique one and cooed appreciatively over it, testing her strength against the tension of the string.

The Paris Trinity, meanwhile, had gone to a smaller cabinet right by the door. Francine strapped a belt full of throwing knives across her chest, while Coralie pulled out a wicked-looking, glinting stiletto knife and strapped it to her thigh. Henri opened their long, gothic black coat and I saw that a long sheath had been concealed in the lining. They picked up one of the silver rapiers Isobel had been admiring and sheathed it inside their coat.

'So,' I said, 'this your first demon fight as a Trinity, isn't it?'

The three of them looked at each other and nodded.

'We 'ave been training, but it is ...' Francine began.

'What was yours like?' asked Henri, nervously running their fingers over the shape of the rapier beneath their coat.

I let out my breath as a sort of half-laugh. '*Well*,' I said. 'It was a little ... we were quite ... We were in a total panic,' I admitted. I cast a glance at Isobel, wondering if she would approve of me being so candid, but her expression wasn't giving anything away. 'The demon had kidnapped my father. He got the twins, too. I managed to free them, but by that point we were tired and beaten up, and Kincaid had nearly cut my head off ...'

'Wow,' said Coralie, wide-eyed. I couldn't help but smile at the idea that anyone could possibly look up to *us* as trained, experienced Demon Hunters – but I guess compared to these three, who'd bonded days ago and hadn't ever been in a real fight, we seemed like veterans. I was suddenly very, very glad that Eva and Isobel would both be with us when we went to the bridge.

In the other corner of the room, Minerva picked up a crossbow bolt and there was a flash as lightning flew from her fingers and crackled up and down its length for a few seconds.

'Woooooow,' said Coralie again. 'Your powers are so fantastic! Strength, lightning, and a Seer! What a combination.'

'What about you guys?' Vesta asked. 'We know you're fast – what about Francine and Henri?'

'Franci is Wolverine,' said Henri. I turned to stare at her.

'Not the claws,' said Francine hurriedly. 'The healing.'

'Oh. Oh but *wow*,' I said. 'You mean you can't get hurt? That must be amazing!'

'It is extremely rare. And it is ... very good,' Francine said, although she sounded a little dubious. 'But it does not mean I can't get hurt, only that I do not remain hurt. I cannot practise it. It only ... *'appens*.'

'And Henri?' Vesta asked.

Henri looked slightly embarrassed. I saw them cast a glance at Eva. For a second, I wondered if they *didn't* have any powers ... but then they sighed and began to float gently upwards.

I looked down at their feet. There was nothing underneath them. Nothing at all.

Despite the fact that *all* of this was provably, definitely real magic, I still had the urge to pat them down looking for hidden wires.

'You can *fly*?' Vesta gasped. '*Dude*, I mean ... *dude*.'

'On my sixteenth birthday, I was skiing back home in the village. I took a ski jump, and just ... kept going,' Henri said, touching gracefully back to earth. 'There is not much use for it in ordinary life,' they added ruefully. 'Not in the city.'

'I bet,' I said, finally picking my jaw up off the floor. 'Must make changing light bulbs easy, though.'

'Yes,' Henri giggled. 'That is true.'

'Diana, have you found a weapon yet?' Isobel prompted me.

'Oh! No, I – sorry, I'll find something.'

I gave the Paris Trinity a last grin and turned back to the racks of weapons. I picked up an axe and then thought about the sharp blade of the Maiden, about Kincaid's obsession with cutting off heads, and I decided to put it down again.

'Eva,' Minerva said, shouldering a crossbow and a quiver full of bolts. 'Do you mind if I ask what happened to the Dragon's vessel? The human it possessed to get into our world?'

'Well done, Minerva, I was waiting for one of you to ask that question,' said Isobel, and shook her head. 'I can see that we will need to do some basic metaphysics revision when we get home.'

I suppressed a groan. When she said revision, she wasn't kidding. I saw an exam in my future.

'It is . . . unknown whether there ever was a vessel,' Eva said.

'But I thought demons couldn't come into this world without possessing someone?' I frowned. 'How come it can manifest like it does?'

'Probably the vessel was destroyed,' said Isobel sharply. 'Though we aren't sure how.'

'*Or,*' Eva insisted, 'there might be another explanation.'

I looked from Eva's raised eyebrows to Isobel's sceptical frown and back again, getting the distinct feeling that I'd blundered into a level of Demon Hunter academics I was not entirely prepared for. Isobel sighed.

'Indeed, there are . . . stories,' she said, turning to admire a gleaming Roman breastplate and helmet in a glass case. 'Of demons who found a way to manifest in our world, in their true form.'

'The legend calls them Harbingers,' said Eva. 'They leave behind a sort of trail that other demons can easily follow into our world.'

'*Legend* is the operative word,' said Isobel. 'The ways of demons can be strange, but I don't believe I've ever seen proof that these Harbingers exist.'

'Well, I've reached out to every Demon Hunter I have contact with,' Eva went on. 'The Athenian Harpies, the Soo family, the Abenaki – Mrs Carter, of course – *all* of the Scandinavians. In the past few weeks, I have written or spoken to several more Demon Hunters than I even knew existed. Not a single one of them knows who destroyed the Dragon's vessel.'

I shuddered. It was incredible to think there were so many other Demon Hunters out there in the world, lineages we had never met or heard of, fighting their own battles. But at the same time, a horrible thought struck me – what if Oriax wasn't lurking around Edinburgh waiting for us to find and kill it after all? What if, like the Dragon might have done, it'd flown off in his true form to some distant part of the world, maybe somewhere they didn't even *have* a Trinity?

There were plenty of places in the world where a demon who fed on hateful murders like Kincaid's would feel right at home ...

'I feel the origin of the Dragon is a problem we can continue to work on after we have destroyed the demon itself,' Isobel said, a little pointedly.

I was still the only one without a weapon. I looked around, still not sure what I should choose if I couldn't have a spear or a staff – and my gaze fell on the crafting bench with its cabinet of ingredients, and then on the bows in one corner. I picked up a quiver and tested the tip of an arrow on my finger.

'Eva,' I said. 'Is there any sulphur in those drawers?'

CHAPTER NINE

The one advantage *le Dragon Rouge* had given us was that where the fog lay so heavy you couldn't see beyond arm's length, you could move about almost without seeing or being seen by a soul.

I had never visited Paris before, and it didn't feel like I was really there now either. I knew we'd passed by several of the landmarks and tourist spots I'd want to hit up if I was on holiday. I knew, as we easily slipped by the police barricade and stepped on to the Pont d'Iéna, that the huge Trocadéro Gardens were behind me and the actual Eiffel Tower itself was right ahead. I should have been looking up at it, but there wasn't even a shadow. It was the middle of the day but Paris was silent, an unreal movie backlot version of the riotous city I had heard about.

The flowers for the dead were even worse in person.

They weren't hundreds of bunches deep, like the memorials you usually saw on TV, at the home of a celebrity or the site of a mass tragedy – but they went on and on, a few every couple of feet, all across the bridge. I forced myself not to look at the photos or read the messages on the drooping signs.

On the way back, I told myself. *After we've destroyed the demon, you can come here, and grieve for all of these people, and feel all of these feelings.*

Right now, I had a job to do.

All the others seemed to feel the same, except for Minerva. She was reading the signs closely as she passed.

'Head in the game, Min,' Vesta muttered.

'It is. I want to know their names,' Minerva replied. 'I want to know who I'm fighting for.'

Eva and Isobel had gotten ahead of us, and they loomed out of the fog as we caught up.

'All right, girls,' said Isobel, as all six of us gathered around them. 'We'll use both of your formations to blast away this fog. If the demon is here, perhaps we will catch him, or perhaps he will be drawn to us, ready for battle. Either way, you must be ready.'

'Vesta, you go across the road with Coralie,' said Eva, gesturing roughly towards three equal points around the bridge. 'Francine with Minerva on this side about ten paces, Diana with Henri back the other way. Isobel and I will stand by with the sulphur gun. *Bonne chance, mes amis.*'

The Paris Trinity all put their hands over their hearts, and then they went in for a group hug, kissing Eva's cheeks at least three times each. It was the Frenchest thing I'd

123

ever seen. Isobel stood relaxed and dignified beside them – not judging their unfiltered affection, but making it very clear that she didn't invite such a thing from us.

I was glad to be paired with Henri. If something went wrong – not that it was going to, but, if it did, if I wasn't as free of the Dragon's control as Isobel and Eva seemed to think . . . I believed that I would be safe with Henri.

We headed down the road side by side, counting ten paces, and when we turned to face the others, they were only dim shapes in the fog.

'Ready?' I asked Henri.

'I do not know. Probably not,' they replied, and then smiled down at me.

'Ha! Girl after my own heart,' I muttered. 'Me neither.'

We stood there for a moment, waiting for something to happen. Nothing did.

'You think that we should – *oh.*' Henri straightened up. 'Never mind,' they said faintly.

Watching the formation take hold from the outside was very strange. I thought I could feel the power radiating off Henri. They straightened up, lips slightly parted, eyes fixed on the middle distance, their hand raised, the glowing purple mark peeking out from under the cuffs of their coat. A wavering suggestion of moving air connected them to Coralie and to Francine, linked heart to heart.

Suddenly I shuddered, hard, feeling as if something intangible had just passed through me. My feet moved almost without any input from my brain. They knew they weren't where they should be, and sure enough I stepped aside and everything dropped away as I felt myself connect

124

to Minerva and to Vesta. I couldn't see them, but I could feel their energies. And I could feel our net of power, the invisible lines snapping into place between us. At once, the fog between us boiled away and the air began to clear. Two triangles were clearly more powerful than one, and where they overlapped, the fog was already gone ...

But something was wrong. I grimaced and rolled my shoulders, uncomfortable. Something was making me feel like my vertebrae were grinding together, like an imperceptibly quiet but almost unbearable feedback sound was playing just behind my eyeballs.

I had to move. And not because the demon was telling me to – this was *us*, doing this, doing something wrong ...

There was no demon on the bridge, as the fog cleared from the vibrating air between us. Only an empty patch of road, bathed in pale November sunshine. I could see the mingled disappointment and relief on the faces of Minerva, Francine, Vesta and Coralie, and then I saw them sag as I stepped out of formation. They'd been feeling that horrible sensation too. The twanging power lines, holding them so close together, it felt *wrong*. How could that be, though – weren't we supposed to be able to work together? The thought formed an ice-cold ball of sadness at the back of my throat.

'*Qu'est-ce que c'est?*' Henri gasped. 'What was?'

'I don't—' I began, but then I saw Vesta and Coralie's heads snap up at the same time, and followed their gazes.

There was a figure. Something walking through the fog, along the bridge towards us. It was vaguely man-shaped ... my fingers flexed and my hand twitched up to take an arrow from the quiver strung across my back. Then I let it fall back, a relieved sigh misting the cold air in front of my face.

There were no wings, no claws. It wasn't even the police, just an ordinary man in a tracksuit who looked like he was out for a run.

He stepped into the clearing of sunlight and stared at the eight of us. Vesta and Coralie immediately tried to act natural, as if they'd just happened to be out here chatting, with crossbows strapped to their backs, when the fog just happened to part around them. Neither of them were very good at 'natural', but they were giving it their best shot. Minerva and Francine were doing the same, and I couldn't see Eva or Isobel ...

Which was why it was only Henri and I who seemed to notice that the man continued to stare, blankly, as if he couldn't care less how suspicious or armed we were. Was I imagining it, or was his face a little too red, his eyes glinting strangely in the ...

He turned, and headed for the railing.

'He's going to jump!' I yelled, and leaped into a full-on sprint towards the rail. The man climbed up, cast a look back at me.

He *smiled*. And then he jumped.

I thought, *There's nothing I can do, he's probably broken his spine on the water, he's going to drown, he's dead already.*

But I didn't stop running.

There is something I can do.

I can dive.

I dropped everything I was holding. I threw off my

coat and I kicked off my shoes. Behind me I heard the others yelling – something about the water, something about the shore – and then I was over the rail, hands over my head, arcing down into the *what the hell am I doing I must be ins—*

The water hit me like a ten-tonne truck made out of freezing cold. I plunged down, blind and desperate for breath. For a few seconds in the murky darkness the cold water seemed to get right into my skull and all thoughts and feelings were wiped away. I bluescreened like an old computer.

Just barely, I remembered to swim. My head broke the surface and I swore and gasped, flailing around, searching for the man who'd jumped.

I couldn't see him.

'*Il est là!*' came a voice from over my head. 'There, Diana!'

I looked up. Henri was hovering just over the water, goth coat billowing around them, and pointing. I followed the gesture, and saw something grey floating on the dark brown surface of the river. It was the man's tracksuit jacket.

I dived under it and my searching hands found something soft and cold. I dragged it towards me, up to the surface, my shoulder singing with pain as I tugged with all my might and the cold Seine started to work its way through my bandage and across the claw-mark.

The man's face broke the surface and I scrambled to keep it there. I couldn't tell if he was alive. He didn't seem to be awake. I hooked his arm over my shoulder and started to struggle towards the shore, kicking out with my legs again and again.

I wouldn't be dragged under. I wouldn't let him drown. I'd already *done* the stupid thing, it was too late for regrets now, I *had* to make it …

I heard a splash over by the shore. It wasn't actually so much a shore as a concrete footpath that ran along the side of the river and under the bridge. Figures swam towards me, one moving strong and steady as a shark, the other shooting across the water like a rocket, kicking up spray behind her.

Coralie got to me first and shoved her small shoulder underneath mine, then Vesta reached us, her golden hair hanging down over her face in strings like a Japanese ghost. She lifted the man off both of us and struck out for the shore, holding him out of the water.

'Hold on,' said Coralie, getting behind me, and before I could ask what was happening she had started to kick her legs again, and now both of us were being propelled towards the path so fast that I yelped and got a mouthful of river water, and I had to put out my hands to catch the concrete coming towards me, or I could've broken my nose.

Hands hooked under my shoulders and I felt myself lifted out of the water and deposited on the blessedly solid path.

Henri's feet in their purple DMs alighted gently beside my head and I felt hands helping me sit up, patting me on the back.

'OK? Anything broken?' asked Coralie. I couldn't speak, but I shook my head.

Vesta rolled the man on to the concrete next to me, and rose out of the water with a single shove on the edge of the shore, throwing back her hair, instantly transforming from Sadako into the Little Mermaid, if Ariel had gone swimming in filthy river water in the middle of November with a full complement of hunting knives still strapped to her.

Minerva, Isobel, Eva and Francine all came clattering down the steps on to the concrete platform. Isobel went straight to the man and started to pump on his chest. A sputter of water fountained out of his mouth but he didn't wake up.

'The ambulance is coming,' Francine said, pocketing her phone.

'He's alive, just about,' said Isobel, running her hands over his pelvis and down his legs. 'Both the legs are broken, I think, and he's out cold from the shock – but he might live. Thanks to you girls. Now, Diana, are you listening to me?'

I tried to focus on her face. I guess I was a little shocky myself. I was freezing, and soaked, my clothes clinging to me. 'I'm OK. I'm listening.'

'That was *incredibly stupid*,' Isobel said. 'And incredibly brave. Don't you dare risk your life like that again.'

Mixed messages, Auntie, I thought, still a little dazed. 'Yes, Isobel,' I said out loud.

Between the five dry Demon Hunters and three wet ones, we managed to orchestrate a swap so that everyone had *something* dry to wear. I ended up wearing Minerva's hat and gloves. It could've been worse. But then, it could have been better – a small brown-ish blur shot out of the fog and passed me, trailing steam, and then it went back the other way. Soon Coralie skidded to a halt beside me, her hair and blouse almost completely dry.

I wasn't sure how long it took the ambulance to arrive, but it seemed to come very quickly. Isobel had Vesta, Coralie and me hide from the paramedics around the corner until they'd intubated the man and taken him away on a stretcher, loading him into the ambulance and rushing off with its strange French sirens blaring. I thought of James Armstrong again – this was the second time in less than twenty-four hours I hadn't gone to hospital when I would have advised any ordinary person to go straight to the ER. What was his reasoning? What had he been hiding? Or had he just not wanted to get in trouble with school?

Well, if that was the case, wandering around Holyrood Park covered in blood was a funny way to go about it ...

As soon as the ambulance was gone, Isobel and Eva started talking in half-English, half-French, half-whispers about what we would do now, whether we should try somewhere else or lie in wait here.

'The cluster around here could just have been because it's a convenient place to kill oneself,' said Isobel bluntly. 'As we've seen.'

'I suppose you are right.' Eva frowned and ran her hands through her sleek black bob. 'Still, its *influence* was here; that poor man did jump. I would be surprised if the demon strayed far from its victims. It must enjoy their suffering ...'

I shuddered and looked up at the bridge, watching the fog slowly close back over the space we'd made.

It was moving very strangely – instead of the drifting bank of earthbound cloud gradually and randomly spreading out to fill the space, a slow but distinct stream of fog was being drawn across the clear space and down over the side of the bridge, towards the path we were standing on.

Where was it going? Was there some kind of air current there, coming from underneath the bridge? I stepped closer, squinting and tilting my head, trying to see if the fog was drawn to the water – no, it wasn't that.

I closed my eyes and held out my hand, stepping carefully forward, trying to feel the air around me.

There was a breeze, but perhaps it was *just* a breeze? It was November and I was under a bridge, it could've been ...

'Diana, what are you doing?' asked Isobel's voice. I opened my eyes and looked back at the others, who were all staring at me.

'Probably nothing,' I shrugged. 'The way the fog's moving. It's like it's all flowing to ...' I waved my arms in a wide gesture that took in the path underneath the bridge. 'Somewhere here. I don't know. It's probably nothing ...'

But as I moved my hands, one of them passed through a patch of air that was *definitely* different to the others. The breeze was much more intense, right there, and wetter – as if the fog was condensing down to flow through a small space. I put my hand out again and yes, I was right.

I peered, trying to follow the line of fog. I must have looked crazy, at least to a normal person – the other girls gathered around curiously, taking this at least as seriously as I was doing.

'What is that?' said Francine.

'What, where?' I said, not looking at her, afraid to take my eyes off the thin stream of water droplets I'd spotted in case I couldn't find them again. I followed them along, and they suddenly ... stopped. 'No, wait, I found it.'

Hanging in the air, there was a ... a something. It wasn't like the portal that'd brought us to Paris, which had been like a full-on tear in the fabric of reality, a wavering line of light. This was more like a pinprick, only visible because of the way it distorted things around it. The fog was flowing into it.

All things considered, I really should have known better than to touch it.

Maybe it was the shock of the cold water still rattling my senses, or the excitement at having found it at all, but my toddler hindbrain somehow bypassed every self-preservation instinct I had, and I touched it.

'It's – *no!*' Isobel shouted.

Too late.

When I was thirteen, I'd broken my ankle at ju-jitsu class. I could feel it now, not the sharp, shocky pain of the moment it happened, but the much worse throbbing agony of the drive to the hospital.

I thought my head was going to explode as every headache I'd ever had came back, all at once. Every stitch and cramp I'd ever endured. The rasping pain in my throat from every bout of flu.

Every kick that had ever landed hard when I was sparring in class. Every punch Kincaid or Alex had landed on me. The time he'd dragged me by my hair.

Every papercut, every stubbed toe. Every spine-crushing period cramp.

The pain I'd felt in visions: the agony of Isobel burning at the stake, the unbearable, unrelenting pricking of Kincaid's needle on the flesh of the women he'd tortured.

I knew all of it, felt all of it. My world was black, timeless, nameless. I didn't know gravity or air, but I knew even through the blinding hurt that *that* sensation was the chunk I'd taken out of my knee falling off my bike, and *that* was Skeevy Steve's hand tightening on my wrist, and *that* . . .

I heard distant screaming. I opened my eyes, and through a red haze I caught a glimpse of something . . . a landscape, maybe. It was scarred and blackened. Shapes jutted up, like broken bones sticking through flesh.

Then I felt the cold and damp hit my face like a slap with a soft, wet towel. I was lying on hard, cool concrete with two pairs of hands holding my head and my wrists. Vesta and Minerva. They must have grabbed me as I slipped – in? through? I wasn't sure – and dragged me back away from the hole in the world.

The pain was gone, but the memory of it wasn't. I gasped in a breath of cool, foggy Paris air and screamed. I couldn't hold it in or keep it quiet – I wailed like a toddler for a full minute, and then I blacked out.

I don't think I was out long. I woke up propped against the underside wall of the bridge.

I was . . . fine. I turned my head and rolled my shoulders against the cool, damp stone, reorienting myself in the real world. My hands were shaking a little, but I wasn't in pain, just . . .

'Don't touch it!' I gasped. 'Everybody get back!'

'It's all right,' Isobel said gently, kneeling beside me and taking my hand. 'Nobody's going to touch it. Diana, can you tell me what you saw?'

' . . . I didn't . . . I felt . . . ' I shook my head, the words just not coming. I stared out over the foggy surface of the Seine and tried to think. What *had* I seen? 'It was . . . a place. I think. Red and black and all churned up. There were . . . I don't know, trees, rocks, buildings? I don't know. I couldn't see, it hurt . . . '

Isobel's grip on me changed, becoming firmer and softer at the same time. She stroked the top of my hand with her thumb. 'You poor child,' she whispered. 'You poor, brave girl.'

I blinked up at her, nervous of this softness. *You're very brave – never do that again* was much more Isobel's style. This was pure sympathy, and I didn't like it.

'I think you saw the demon world, Diana.'

Coralie gasped and made a gesture, blurred with speed, that I realised must have been crossing herself.

'A doorway to the demon dimension,' Isobel went on, shaking her head. 'I've read of such things, and the pain they cause any human who tries to pass through . . . I never thought I would live to see it.'

Tears sprang to my eyes again, but I tried to blink them away, and nodded.

'It explains so much. Eva – you were right,' Isobel said, looking over her shoulder. 'The Dragon has no vessel; it never did have one. A Harbinger demon brings more demons in its wake, correct?'

I peered up at Eva. She looked frozen, as if she was afraid to move, but finally she nodded. 'That is what I have heard.'

I slowly turned to look back at the pinprick, or where I thought it was – oh God, I couldn't see it any more. I tried to stamp down the rising panic at the thought that someone might walk into it by accident. 'It opened a tear in reality. It didn't need to be invited? And ... and *more* of them can come through that tiny gap?'

'That sounds bad,' said Vesta.

'It is bad,' said Isobel. She turned and looked at Eva, whose face had turned a sickly green now. 'Very bad indeed.'

I sat up, feeling a little stronger, but before I could ask what we could do about it, there was a sound from up above us.

A scream that pierced the air before fading to a gurgling moan.

Isobel leaped to her feet, looked up, then glanced back down at me.

'Go! Jeez,' I snapped, waving her away as I struggled slowly to my feet.

The French Trinity had already gone, Coralie in a puff of swirling fog, Francine and Eva pounding up the concrete stairs, Henri leaping into the air and vanishing into the fog. Isobel and Minerva followed, but Vesta waited.

She held out a hand to me and pulled me gently to my feet, then she threw an arm around my shoulders, letting me use her as a full-body crutch.

'Go as slow as you need, the French've got this,' she murmured as we headed for the steps.

'I'm OK,' I told her, but I held on tight. I didn't really need the physical support, but she was warm and solid.

By the time we had climbed the stairs to the bridge and jogged unsteadily to the middle of the bridge, the Paris Trinity were in formation, the fog roiling between them. Isobel and Eva were kneeling on the pavement, busy hands holding and tending to a woman who lay against the railing. Blood was pouring from her chest and had spattered across a bunch of lilies she'd been holding.

She'd been slashed across her front, as if with a knife – or a giant claw.

'*Le Dragon Rouge*,' Eva gasped, as she saw us coming. 'It is here!'

CHAPTER TEN

Vesta didn't want to let me go, but I pushed her away. 'Triangle, now! They've got it, but we have to back them up.'

Minerva was already in place, and Vesta and I staggered into formation.

It was the Dragon in their net, all right. The fog was sucking and curling in on itself, starting to take form. A pair of sweeping fog wings beat and twitched, their span somehow even larger than I remembered.

I stood beside Francine, and our triangle snapped into place – but I got that feeling again, as if someone was dragging their nails down the blackboard of my soul.

One of the great grey wings lashed out, and it struck the place where our triangle overlapped with theirs. The vibration slammed into me, almost knocking me out of position. I clutched instinctively at my chest – my heart felt like someone had driven a bass guitar string right through and then plucked it hard.

We were weak. Right where we should have been strong. Tears of frustration sprang to my eyes – I just didn't *understand* it!

The grey figure at the centre of our triangles writhed and flailed with its wings again, striking the crossover between Henri and Vesta on one point and Coralie and Minerva on the other – I felt it again, like a full-body slap, but Coralie actually staggered. She snapped back into place, but her shoulders were shaking.

Seams of red started to appear through the swirling fog that still covered the Dragon's body.

'You have it,' Isobel said somewhere behind me. 'You've nearly got it, just don't move!'

I tried to root my feet in the stones of the bridge and hold on, but the grating feeling was growing, right at the base of my neck.

Why would it do this? Why wouldn't two triangles be better than one? What are we doing wrong?

It struck me just as the Dragon was winding up to lash out at the edges of its prison again.

'The power's not flowing right, it's not ... *equal*,' I said to Francine.

'*Oui*,' she said through gritted teeth.

Equal triangles, equal distances ...

'We have to make a star!' I shouted. 'Paris stay put, twins with me, move around.'

138

I could see it in my mind's eye, as if I was looking down from space – so perfect, so obvious, I couldn't understand why we hadn't been doing it all along. I stepped further away from Francine, positioning myself between her and Henri, and the twins moved too. The triangle shifted, overlapping theirs, snapping into place.

All six of us gasped. Something seemed to shoot between us, along the lines of power – a fizzing spark, blue as a gas flame.

It felt so *good*. I felt like I could run a marathon, climb a mountain, fight an army. I grinned and unsheathed the knife I'd attached to my belt. I hadn't had a chance to pick up my bow since I'd dropped it to launch myself into the river, but Minerva, Henri and Francine all still had theirs. They pulled them out, notching the sulphur-dipped bolts and arrows to their strings.

'Get ready. Fire on my word!' cried Eva.

The Dragon roared, that sound like metal screaming against metal, and its wings turned red and solid. It looked even weirder in the light of day. The smooth redness of its skin ... the whites of its eyes ...

It turned them on me, and I raised my chin and stared right back.

Try me, you bastard. I know your tricks and I'm ready for you: just try *me!*

The Dragon turned away, its wings trembling with rage. I grinned in triumph, feeling smug and powerful, ready to see it riddled with arrows. It turned, as if searching for a way out of its trap. There was none. We had it ...

But suddenly it stopped, and folded its wings, and looked right at Coralie.

She crossed herself again with a shaking hand, but even as she did so, her other hand was drawing her stiletto knife from its sheath, turning it so the point of the blade was aimed at herself, right at her heart.

'Cora!' Francine screamed.

'Coralie, no!' yelled Henri.

'No,' said Coralie in a thin voice. 'No, I won't, I won't . . .'

The blade trembled and wavered in her hand, but it drew itself back, ready to plunge into her chest.

'Fire!' Eva yelled.

Minerva shot first, a crackling sulphur-and-lightning bolt catching the Dragon in the head, right behind one pointed, bat-like ear. It screamed.

Painfully slowly, Coralie's fingers uncurled, and she dropped the knife. It clattered to the ground at her feet. Her hands came up in front of her, as if she was trying to claw at her own skin, yet also trying not to. She let out a moan of terror.

Henri let loose an arrow that struck the Dragon in the ribs. Francine shot one right through its wing. The arrow ripped a steaming hole right through the thin, red membrane, hit the road beyond and clattered away.

'Over here, demon!' Isobel cried. It spun to face her, opened its mouth and screamed with rage again. She levelled her pistol, took aim, and fired. A spark and a puff of smoke rose from the pistol, and the Dragon staggered back as part of its chest exploded. Thick chunks of demon flesh flew off in all directions. Some landed sizzling on the ground at our feet.

'Get it, girls!' commanded Eva.

Francine stepped out of formation first. She sprinted to Coralie, grabbed one of her wrists, and pulled her into a tight hug. '*Vas-y!*' she said. '*Vous pouves le faire, il suffit de respirer ...!*'

Minerva and Henri fired again, and another sulphurous arrow and crackling crossbow bolt buried themselves in the demon's flesh. The rest of us advanced on the Dragon, blades drawn. The demon tried to lash out at us with its wings and claws, but we ducked and wove and stabbed.

One of its arms caught Vesta on the backswing, sharp spines snagging on her clothes, but it was already weak and the points of its spines only scratched her. Vesta caught its arm in one of hers and bent it around backwards.

'Got you now!' she crowed, raising her knife and driving it deep into the Dragon's back. The demon screamed again, and managed to throw her off. She hit the concrete hard, but rolled and staggered to her feet, her teeth bared in a bloody grin.

I ducked just in time to avoid a scything wing at head height, then twisted and aimed a sweeping kick at the Dragon's legs. It went down, more ashy red chunks breaking off it as its knees hit the ground.

A crossbow bolt struck it right in the centre of its bullet wound, and the Demon roared and fell backwards, twitching. I looked up to see Minerva grinning a wild and violent grin.

Henri sent another sulphuric arrow into the Dragon's

chest, and Minerva winched back the crossbow string and got it right under the chin.

The Dragon lay still.

'The head!' Isobel cried, sounding out of breath. I turned and saw that she and Eva were barely even watching our fight – they were both hunched over the bleeding woman, packing her wound with torn strips of cloth, compressing her heart to keep it beating. 'Take the head.'

Vesta had the largest cutting knives of any of us. I looked to her, but then I saw her watching Coralie. The French girl was approaching the demon, shaking, but also holding Francine's hand and no longer trying to hurt herself.

Vesta turned the knife around in her hand and held it out to Coralie.

Wordlessly, Coralie took it.

Was that a good idea?

But I needn't have worried. Coralie knelt by the demon's neck and brought her knife down in a hard, workmanlike series of strikes, until the Dragon's head rolled away.

The moment the final strings of matter had been severed, the fog around us began to lift. I stood and went to the railing of the bridge, staring as Paris unveiled itself in front of me. Buildings began to appear, and a few cars. A few people who'd braved the dangers of the fog watched in wonder as it vanished before their eyes. The sun came out, and the green-brown waters of the Seine glittered. I looked up, and there was the Eiffel Tower, curving iron girders perfect and gleaming. There were giant horse-plus-naked-man statues on enormous plinths at either end of the bridge. We must have walked past them several times.

'Hey, look,' said Minerva, sounding dazed. 'We killed a demon. And we're in Paris!'

CHAPTER ELEVEN

'Hey, hey, Diana, hey!' Coralie appeared at my elbow, out of nowhere. 'Two more mochas and two cakes, with ginger.' She dropped some euros on the bar, and vanished again. I blinked over the bar at the café owner, wondering if I was going to have to explain my friend's teleportation trick to him, but he didn't seem to have noticed.

I managed to order drinks and cake – due to his English being impeccable rather than to my French being in any way adequate – and juggled them back to the table by the window, where the girls were deep in what looked like a very important conversation.

'No, no, no,' Francine was saying. 'I am sorry, Minerva, you are wrong. The best house is *obviously* Slytherin.'

Minerva let out a mocking laugh. 'Really. *Really?* They sleep in a dungeon!'

'It is a beautiful dungeon.'

'I bet it smells of damp and snakes.'

'Snakes do not even *have* a smell, unlike scruffy old *ravens . . .*'

I passed around the mugs and plates of cake, and settled down in a chair opposite Henri, sipping my coffee, savouring the taste as it hit the back of my tongue.

'Are you dry now?' Henri asked, taking a big sip of a hugely frothy hot chocolate.

'Not quite,' I said, resisting the urge to wriggle in my seat – I knew full well that rearranging the collection of sticky wrinkles that were my underwear and my shirt would not actually make anything better. 'But I am warm.'

'That was incredible, you know. The dive into the Seine.'

I smiled and blushed. 'Isobel was right, it was very stupid. But I'm glad I did it.'

I looked around at the other Demon Hunters, chatting and laughing. Then I looked out through the café window. It was dark outside now, and the lights of the buildings along the Seine were softly reflected on the water.

'Can you believe we killed a demon?' Henri said softly. 'Truly killed one?'

'Not really,' I shook my head. 'It's gone, and it's never coming back.'

'Not after what we did,' said Henri.

I nodded, shuddering a little. Coralie had suggested that since I hadn't had the chance to cut off the head of the Dragon, I should get to be the one to post it back to its demon brothers on the other side of the dimensional doorway. I appreciated the thought, but when the process was over I decided I would have preferred to burn it or sink it far out to sea. Instead of being ripped out of my hands all in one go, holding it up to the dimensional hole seemed to *shred* the body of the demon, turning it into a sort of thin soup and sucking it away, as had happened with the fog.

I took another sip of coffee and tried not to think about the demon too hard. Isobel had been right, this *was* better than the pigs. The Dragon had been pure evil, and it wasn't remorse I was feeling, just pure, A-grade *squick*.

Coralie and Vesta were playing some kind of game of spinning coins between goalposts made out of pepper pots, and Francine and Minerva had moved on to arguing about some other books which I didn't think I'd read, but then Francine broke off as her phone started to bleep and vibrate on the table in front of her. She picked it up and flicked to her messages.

'It's from Eva,' she said, and we all held our breath. 'The lady on the bridge is going to be OK!'

We all cheered and raised our mugs.

'*Santé*,' said Francine.

'Cheers,' I said.

'*Air do slainte*,' said Minerva, with a cheeky grin on her face. 'Gaelic,' she explained, and the Paris Trinity laughed.

There was a lull in the conversation as we all drank deeply, thanking a variety of powers that we had saved a life, and that there would be no more flowers along the Pont d'Iéna, at least not for a while. No more pictures and cardboard hearts.

Grace. Martin. Levoy. Ivy. Gideon. Rishi.

I'd gone back. I'd read the names, looked at the photographs, allowed myself to wish we could have done more. I didn't linger very long. It felt like something I needed to do, to wring the grief out of my heart, as I'd wrung the water of the Seine from my hair – but it wasn't *for* me.

'What do you think Isobel and Eva wanted to talk about all by themselves?' Coralie asked.

'I'm guessing the hole to the demon world,' I said, glad to talk about something else.

Eva had suggested that the six of us go out this evening, to celebrate our first kill and to get to know each other, and I for one was hugely glad that she had. But we all knew there was more to it. After we'd gotten rid of the body, Isobel had told Eva that they needed to talk, and Eva had got that slightly sick look again.

'How are we going to close it? I mean, we *have* to close it, don't we?' Minerva said. 'Or else a bunch more demons can just come through, right?'

'We will kill them all!' announced Coralie, wielding a spoon like dagger.

'*Oui*,' said Henri, a lot more cautiously. 'But Minerva is right, if we can close it, we must.'

We all nodded. I just hoped that Isobel and Eva knew how we would do it, because I wasn't going near that thing. Not ever again.

'Listen, Henri,' Vesta said, leaning over her ginger cake. 'Real talk. Are you *she*? Or *they*? Or one of the weird ones like *ze*?'

I flushed slightly, hoping that Henri wouldn't take offence at Vesta's bluntness.

To my relief, Henri smiled shyly. 'It is a little complex. I am . . . not . . . *fixed*. You know? I like the English "they". In French, it is harder.'

'That's right,' said Minerva, frowning as if she'd remembered something. 'There's not really a gender-neutral pronoun in French, not even like "they". Literally everything in French is gendered one way or the other, right, that's just how the grammar works.'

The Paris Trinity all nodded and shrugged and made 'well, kind of' motions with their hands. I guessed this was the closest we were going to get without taking a couple of intensive language courses.

Vesta turned her attention back to Henri. 'So what happened? How did you realise you were, *you know* . . . a Demon Hunter?'

'*Je suis désolé, ma sœur est très terrible*,' said Minerva. 'I can make her stop if you want.' But Henri laughed.

'It is OK. As I said, my powers came to me on my sixteenth birthday. I already knew I was not a boy, but I had not come out to my mother yet – once you have flown through the air, though, you know *something* is up! We were a Demon Hunter family, and my mother knew that these two had been born on the same day, but she didn't think to tell me until I came out to her. Then she sent me here, to meet Eva, and . . . to see what happened.'

'Thank God she did,' said Coralie, grabbing Henri's hands in both of hers. 'We need you!'

Henri grinned. 'I am also glad. Though, if being genderqueer was not 'ard enough,' they said with an impish smile, 'I have to fight demons.'

They shrugged, and I smiled into my coffee. I got the definite impression they weren't finding either all *that* hard.

'And *Henri*?' said Vesta, and Minerva rolled her eyes. 'I mean, don't you want to change it?'

'I am considering,' Henri said, flushing slightly. 'You see, Francine and Coralie were both named out of a book.'

'*The Adventures of Doctor Richars*,' said Francine, with a lopsided smile. 'It is ... what is the word?'

'Pulp,' grinned Coralie.

'Trash,' agreed Henri. 'All of our parents love this silly book. Have you read it?' they asked the girls. Coralie and Francine shook their heads. 'Well, I did. And it turns out that my mother was thinking of it after all. There is no Henri – but there is a Henrietta.'

Coralie gasped and threw her hands up. I realised, with a flash of pride, that this was the first time Henri had said this aloud.

'It is *fate*,' said Coralie. 'Henri, you *must* do it, it is perfect!'

'If it feels like your name,' said Minerva softly.

'It – it really does.' Henri – Henrietta – sat back and sipped their hot chocolate, a quiet, pleased smile on their lips.

'OK,' said Francine, slapping her hands down on to the table. 'Drink up, everybody, and then we are going *dancing. Oui*, yes, we are. Come on, *allons-y*.'

I glanced around, seeing Vesta's eyes light up and Minerva's raise her eyebrows happily.

Well, if Francine insisted, who were we to say no?

Sebastian heard his ringtone and almost fell off his chair, scrambling to scoop his phone out of the pile of miscellaneous cables and books that was stacked on top of his spare computer tower.

'Hello?'

'*Sebastian. It's me. Are they back?*'

It was Alex.

Sebastian bristled slightly. He had handed over his phone number as an empty gesture, under some protest, for emergencies only. Was this an emergency? He highly doubted it.

'No, they're not,' he said.

'*Shit,*' said Alex. '*Well. You'll have to do.*'

'Excuse me, I won't *have to do* anything,' Sebastian said.

Alex paused. '*It's getting worse,*' he said.

Sebastian's heart sank, and not just because he might have to spend yet more time in Alex's company. He remembered the silent school, the doctor, everything Alex had said about the strange behaviour of the students, and he sighed. 'How much worse?'

'Why did we have to meet out here?' Sebastian said, parking Ruby beside the Wallington Services van and getting out. As if Alex wasn't acting suspiciously enough, he'd insisted Sebastian shouldn't drive any closer to the school than the nearest petrol station – the same one they'd pushed Ruby to after the sheep incident.

'I told you,' Alex frowned. 'They've completely closed ranks. Nobody except staff is getting in or out now, not even parents. They told me there's some kind of disease going around – my guess is they actually think Armstrong and his mates have all gone crazy. Either way, they're desperate to keep it out of the press. So, if you want in, you'll have to be staff.' He opened the passenger side door of the van and tossed something blue and gold to Sebastian, who just about managed not to fumble it.

'*Seriously?*' Sebastian complained, holding up the uniform overalls. 'Are these yours? You could get two of me in here.'

'I'll lend you some string for a belt,' said Alex, his lips quirking. Sebastian was certain he was trying not to smile.

Still, at least he was trying.

'This is going to end badly,' Sebastian said, climbing into the van.

Sure enough, the Wallington School gates were shut, but Alex's swipe-card opened them. Sebastian glanced up at the CCTV cameras mounted over the gate.

'Those are new,' he muttered. 'I would have seen them otherwise.'

'They installed them this morning. Seems the Head's finally worked out that some of the boys have been getting out. It was probably you bringing Armstrong back like that that did it.'

There were lights on at the school. The fog seemed to

151

be lifting a little, but in the dark the building still seemed intimidatingly huge.

'Vesta texted me,' Sebastian said. 'She said that they've killed the demon in Paris. She wanted to know if it's solved our problem here too.'

Alex raised an eyebrow. 'I kind of doubt it.'

Me too, Sebastian thought. He reached into the big front pocket of the overalls and turned his phone around and around in his fingers. He had Vesta's new friend Coralie's number. His phone was programmed to ring her if he swiped the wrong passcode – or if the microphone picked up the words *Screw you, Alexander*.

It wasn't that he was afraid. Not of Alex.

He was just being practical.

'I've been tailing Armstrong whenever I can. I heard him and some of his friends talking,' Alex said, parking the van around the back of the school. 'They said they were going to "do it tonight", in the science block. And then they said something I didn't understand.'

'What was it?'

'That's just it, it was like … Latin or Gaelic or something, maybe neither of those. I mean, hell, it could've been Dothraki for all I know, but bottles full of blood and random fainting and speaking in tongues – it all says *demon* to me.'

Sebastian really *wanted* to focus on the demonic activity part, but …

'Dothraki? When have you had time to watch *Game of Thrones*? You've been possessed for the last – however long!'

'Four years,' said Alex, as he turned to get out of the van so quietly Sebastian almost didn't hear him. He slammed the door behind him and Sebastian followed, feeling slightly sick.

He must've been ... what, fourteen? Jeez ...

'Science block's this way. Anyway I was cured months ago, remember?' Alex added lightly. 'What, am I supposed to have been living in a cave since then? Sorry if I'm not acting evil enough for you, it must be very confusing.'

Sebastian followed him across the gravel towards a low, modern-looking annexe that was connected to the main school by a covered walkway. 'Were you this sarcastic when you were possessed?'

'I don't know,' said Alex.

I had to ask. Sebastian shuddered. 'Where are your parents, anyway?'

'No parents.' Alex didn't look at Sebastian. He plunged his hands into his pockets and fixed his gaze on the path in front of him. 'We don't really have time for my life story. I presume I'm still down as a runaway from Saint Cathan's Home for Kids Nobody Wants to Foster. They throw you out at sixteen anyway, so I just got a head start on the sleeping rough part of life. Got my own place now. I really lucked out with this job, or that was what I thought before I started finding ritual sacrifices under the box hedges.'

Sebastian grimaced behind his back. He opened his mouth, then shut it, then opened it again. Should he say something? Should he say *sorry*?

Before he could, Alex held up a hand.

'Shh,' he said, and pushed on the door of the science block. It swung open, and by the look on Alex's face, Sebastian guessed that it wasn't meant to be unlocked.

Or that's what he wants you to think ...

You know what, Sebastian thought, turning on his own inner monologue, *how about you stop being paranoid just for a minute? Something's actually happening here ...*

The inside of the science block smelled strongly of bleach and plastic. The faint light from the school and even fainter moonlight filtered in through the big windows and pooled around the door, but further down the corridor there was pitch darkness.

Sebastian paused, listening. He thought he could hear ... *something*, but he wasn't sure what it was. It could have been the sound of a boiler running, or a computer that'd been left on, or some kind of scientific equipment. It came and went, a soft thrumming sound.

Alex tilted his head towards the end of the corridor, and they advanced into the darkness, going up to the door of each lab in turn, looking for the tell-tale flicker of lights, listening for voices.

There were none, until they came to the very last door. In the pitch black, the line of faint yellow light under the door was like a beacon. Sebastian held his breath, trying to slow his heartbeat so it wouldn't seem so loud in the hissing silence. He thought the thrumming was still there ... or could it just be the sound of his own blood pounding in his head?

Alex's broad shoulders hunched over as he put his ear to the door.

Then Sebastian jumped and almost swore as a voice spoke loudly from behind the door.

'Screw this, I'm leaving.'

A chorus of boys' voices piped up all at once. 'No! Come on, Reid, you can't do this! No!'

'Sit down, Reid, you pussy!' snarled one above the others.

'No way, I'm not doing this any more. It's getting too weird. I'm away to bed.'

Footsteps approached the door. The one Sebastian and Alex were standing right in front of. Sebastian froze – and then Alex had grabbed him and pulled him back against the wall, keeping him back with one arm. They both held their breath.

The door opened.

'Grab him,' said the snarling voice.

Reid didn't make it into the corridor. He let out a yell, and then his voice was muffled and the door was shut again.

Sebastian's heart was racing now, his pulse thumping in his ears.

'What do we do?' he breathed. Alex's eyes widened with panic for a moment, then his gaze flicked from side to side as if he was thinking hard. He held up a hand and gestured for Sebastian to follow him.

He crept to the next lab along, and opened the door slowly. To Sebastian's huge relief, the lab was empty. Grey, shifting moonlight was creeping across the benches and the state-of-the-art equipment. Alex went straight to a door on his right and peered through the large window in its upper half. Sebastian did the same.

Behind the door was a technician's cupboard – a small room that was an organised jumble of boxes and bits of equipment and jars full of things Sebastian really didn't want to look too closely at – and there was another door at the other end, also with a window, through which a flicker of yellow candlelight could just be seen.

Alex opened the door and they crept between the cramped shelves towards the candle-lit lab.

Sebastian did look at the jars. He couldn't help it. Several of the things were entire small creatures. One of them was a large, mammalian head. He regretted looking.

The thrumming was louder now. A sort of buzz, and the odd high-pitched squeak. It was definitely not the muffled voices of the boys in the next room. Was it coming from some bit of equipment in the tech cupboard? Or was it just the pipes, or the central heating cooling at the end of the day? What was that thing they said about noises at night – *it's just the house settling?* Did brand new science blocks settle?

The boys' voices were louder again now. They'd given up on whispering.

'Hold him down, Choudry!' the snarling boy commanded.

Sebastian and Alex crouched down so that they could get to the window without being seen by the boys, and peered into the lab. Sebastian was not particularly surprised to discover that the snarling voice had come from James Armstrong.

One boy, who must be Choudry, was sitting on top of another, who must be Reid, the one who'd tried to leave.

Choudry was pinning Reid's legs, and had his hands clamped over his mouth. There were about eight other boys in the lab, all of them probably in Armstrong's year. It looked like they'd come here from their dorm rooms – several of them were in uniform blue pyjamas, others wearing T-shirts and jeans. Sebastian clocked bandages on at least two hands, and dark bags under some of their eyes. They were sitting in a rough circle, candles at their feet, and something else was glimmering in the flickering light ...

Each boy had a scalpel, and in the middle of the room there was a large, empty glass beaker.

Sebastian felt sick. He turned to Alex, and Alex looked back at him with an infuriating *told you so* kind of expression.

'What are we going to do with him?' asked a voice. Sebastian looked back through the window and saw a ginger boy in uniform pyjamas, fiddling nervously with a scalpel.

'Strip him down and dump him in the pond,' said a pale boy with dark hair, nastily.

'And then call Miss Thomas to bring him a towel,' added another ginger boy, giggling.

'No. No stupid pranks,' said Armstrong. 'This is fate. We said we wanted to make a *real* sacrifice, didn't we? This way we don't have to grab one of the other bugs. The Head already knows Reid's been cutting. He'll think it was suicide.'

'Wait, are you saying ...?' said the nasty dark-haired boy, all the laughter gone from his voice.

'Armstrong,' said a dark-skinned one, 'we can't. Isn't it too soon? You said it was too soon for anything like … like …'

'Power demands sacrifice,' said Armstrong. 'I say let's do it and get it over with.'

The other boys all looked at each other dubiously, and Sebastian felt a flicker of hope – they might be going a little nuts and cutting themselves but they weren't murderers. Not *yet*.

'We all agreed,' said Armstrong, in a reasonable tone of voice. 'Don't you want what we've been promised? Power beyond anything your fathers even dream of?' His voice cracked slightly, and his knee started to jiggle as he talked. 'I've spoken to him. I've seen his face. I know he can do it. Just think about it – what did you ask for?'

The boys all went quiet for a moment, watching the wriggling Reid. Sebastian tried to imagine what they would have asked for, what would be worth *killing* for, and shuddered as one by one they began nodding to themselves.

'I know what I'm asking for,' giggled the ginger one again.

'We all know what you're asking for, Fielding,' teased a thin blond one. 'Any woman you want, any time.'

'You're not thinking big enough,' said the dark-haired one. 'This … thing can change the world. Don't you want them to respect us again? Don't you want them to know their *place*?'

Sebastian shuddered, but when he glanced at Alex, he saw abject *horror* in his face. He looked like he might throw up.

158

'Yeah, that too ...' muttered the ginger one.

'Do you want to end up like one of those sad old men who get so worn down by life that they have to get a gun and shoot up a university just to make their mark?'

The boys all shook their heads.

'You can think as big as you like,' said Armstrong quietly.

And what is it you *want?* Sebastian wondered. *Armstrong is the ringleader – he must have a reason for all this ...*

'You want to change the world? Take it back? You can do it. We just have to make a *sacrifice.*'

They all looked down at Reid again. He was sobbing and trying to get out from under Choudry, but the boy had him pinned down tight.

Alex turned and gripped Sebastian's wrist, so hard that Sebastian had to bite back a yelp. 'Run,' he said. 'Run to the school and get the teachers, get security, get *someone.*'

'What are you going to do?' Sebastian shot back.

'Try not to get stabbed,' Alex said, getting into a crouch with his hands on the door, like a sprinter at the starting block. '*Go.*'

Sebastian scrambled to his feet and ran. He slammed through the doors out of the science block, along the covered walkway and into the main school, pounded down the corridor and skidded out into the main reception area. There was nobody there, but there was a sign to the teachers' quarters, so he put on another burst of speed then started knocking on the first door he came to. There was no answer. The second one opened right away – a man with a bushy beard and an angry expression looked him up and down as if he was mad and very possibly an oik.

'I need help,' Sebastian gasped, his sides aching. 'Call security or something, there are boys in the science block and they've got knives. I think they're going to hurt each other—'

To Sebastian's intense relief, the last few words were said to the man's retreating back as he tied his dressing gown around his waist and stormed off, phone in hand, already dialling.

'It's an *incident*,' he snapped into the handset. 'Yes, another one. Yes! In the science block. Get over there, *now*.'

Still staggering from his sprint over, Sebastian followed the teacher back to the science block. They were met there by two big men in black uniforms, each one armed with what looked like a taser. The bearded man punched the light switch as they entered the block, and Sebastian had to blink to clear his vision as the too-bright light of twenty fluorescent tube bulbs lit up the corridor.

'Boys!' roared the bearded man. 'It's Mr McIntosh, I know you're in there!'

The door to the lab flew open and a couple of the boys spilled out, shouting and pointing.

'Wasn't us, sir . . . '

'I didn't want to be here, sir. Armstrong said . . . '

Sebastian's heart sank.

Oh God – did they kill that kid? Did they kill Alex? *What am I going to tell Diana?*

But then they reached the door to the lab, and there

160

wasn't a huge pool of blood on the floor – there was a cluster of boys shuffling their feet miserably in a corner, Armstrong wielding a scalpel, and Alex standing in front of the door, arms raised.

The next few minutes were a blur of shouting. Armstrong dropped his scalpel at once. More teachers turned up. The boys were marched out of the science block at taser-point. Alex turned out to have one very small cut on his thumb from Armstrong flailing at him. The teacher, McIntosh – who turned out to be the Deputy Head – had a very tense conversation with the doctor, during which Sebastian heard the phrases *medical observation* and *until further notice*.

Then he turned to Sebastian and Alex. 'Thank you,' he said. 'You can go.'

Sebastian knew better than to question it this time.

They passed Armstrong on the way out of the science block. He was being restrained by one of the security guards. Sebastian didn't want to meet his glare, but he couldn't help looking – and he found the boy's eyes red and glistening with frustrated tears. He glared at Sebastian, and then he looked upwards, mouthing something silently, his bottom lip trembling.

Sebastian and Alex both followed his gaze. Sebastian frowned. There was nothing there but the fluorescent ceiling lights, and the clean white tiles ...

... and the hum. There it was again, coming from right above them, the buzzing thrumming sound, punctuated with an occasional *skree* noise, like a hinge that needed oiling.

Sebastian opened his mouth to ask what the hell he was hearing, but then he felt Alex's hand on the back of his neck, fist balling in his shirt.

'Out. Now,' Alex ordered through gritted teeth, and half-dragged him out of the building and across the grass, ignoring the KEEP OFF signs, towards the van. When they got there, Alex opened the driver's side door and then slammed his hand down hard on the bonnet, hard enough that he winced and clutched at his fingers.

'Oh God. We've got to do something, we've got, we've got to . . .' Alex leaned over the bonnet of the van and trailed off.

'Hey,' Sebastian said gingerly. 'What's going on? We stopped him, right? What was that sound? Why are you freaking out all of a sudden?'

'*Why am I freaking out?* I thought you were meant to be the smart one?'

Sebastian bristled, but he didn't have time to retort. Alex cut him off with a look so full of fear and anger that it stole the breath out of his chest.

'I'm *freaking out* because I spent four years with a demon who sounded just like that *living in my head*,' he snarled, pacing the length of the van and back. He reminded Sebastian of a caged tiger. 'I heard the moths. I'm sure I did. Armstrong heard it too, it's Oriax, it's all happening again. All that stuff about power, and sacrifice, and women knowing their place? They're sounding like Kincaid. Like he always sounded, when he'd talk – he would talk, all the time, when he was . . .' Alex twitched, laid his hands on the van as if to steady himself, pushed off and started to

162

pace again. 'I'm freaking out, Seb, because that sounded like *witch-burning* talk to me.'

Sebastian held very still, half afraid that if he moved Alex would just let loose and punch him.

On the plus side, he thought, *if he's really still working for Oriax, the Oscar for best post-traumatic stress performance goes to . . .*

'So,' Sebastian said, and waited for Alex's reaction. Alex stopped pacing again and folded his arms. Sebastian swallowed and went on. 'So they're being watched, now. They're in the medical room, under observation. They won't be able to hurt anyone until they're let out. Right?'

Alex shrugged. 'Maybe.'

'So as soon as the girls get back, we'll fill them in, and we'll decide what to do. If Oriax really is here, we'll need them.'

Alex let out a long breath, and sagged. 'Right. Yeah. You're right. And I'll keep an eye on things and make sure they're not wandering around or murdering each other in the middle of the night. But for God's sake call me as soon as the girls get back, OK?'

'I will.'

'I'm serious.'

Sebastian rolled his eyes. 'So am I. Honestly it's like you think I don't trust you or something. I'll call you.' He slipped into Ruby's driver's seat and started the engine so he didn't have to see the look on Alex's face.

The centre of Paris at night was a beautiful place, the soft and twinkling lights filling every corner and café and bridge with atmosphere and romance, even at 3 a.m. after a really long day and an evening of dancing.

I thought about this as I sat in the back of Eva's van with a small pile of weapons at my feet.

If the police stopped us now, we would be done for terrorism, for sure. But that was why we had to sort this out right now. We'd had about an hour's nap after we got in from our night out with the girls and Henrietta, and now it was time to finish what we started. To close the portal to the demon world, before any more of them came through.

I was a little surprised to hear that Eva and Isobel had a plan already. Given the way they'd spoken to each other earlier, I'd assumed that closing the portal would be a fiendishly difficult job. But Isobel had explained that it would be simple, but dangerous. The six of us were coming as backup only. We would create a power field around the spot, which would stop anything coming through, and make it safe for Eva and Isobel to work. That was *all* we would do, on pain of being seriously glared at.

The fact that Eva and Isobel had chosen to be armed to the teeth anyway seemed ominous, but I tried not to worry about it.

As we slipped out of the van and down the stairs to the path, I gazed up at the Eiffel Tower and the reflections of all the lights dancing in the river. I thought about all those movies where the big romantic reveal happens in Paris, usually somewhere conveniently within sight of the Tower.

These circumstances were … a little different, to be

sure. And perhaps it was only because I was a ridiculous American at heart, still charmed by Hollywood's interpretation of the ancient and mysterious ways of Europe, but I hoped, in that moment, that one day I would get to come here with someone who would be willing to help me live out that fantasy.

Maybe someone who . . .

Well, maybe Alex. It felt redundant to try to fool myself into thinking I could be thinking of anyone else with a chiselled jaw and eyelashes to lift you off your feet. It was silly, sure, but when I let the fantasy play out in front of my eyes, his was the face I saw reflected back at me from the glittering waters of the Seine.

This unscheduled weekend trip to Paris had gone pretty well, considering, but I was looking forward to going home to Edinburgh. I had some unfinished business to get to – I'd find Alex, and I'd make time to talk to Isobel about Mom, and I'd fill Dad in on all this weird new demon mythology. I had a strong feeling that when I told him we'd closed the portal, he would be slightly disappointed . . .

The path under the bridge was dark and chilly. The air coming off the Seine was freezing cold and I wrapped my now-blessedly-dry coat tight around my shoulders.

We laid down the weapons we'd brought with us, and Isobel began to get kitted up. I frowned at the pile, wondering just how many swords, axes and arrows she could possibly need.

She was armed not just to the teeth but all the way up to the top of her head. I frowned at the single stab-proof vest that Eva had on. They must know what they were doing, but it made me uneasy. Perhaps the weapons were all just ceremonial – a kind of visual cue to the demon world that they should think again before trying anything in our reality.

'Girls, come here,' Eva called. She opened her backpack and began to hand out packets of herbs and funny-coloured powders. 'Vesta, come, Isobel says you are good with herbs—'

'The word I used was *competent*,' said Isobel, belting the quiver across her chest. 'You still have a lot to learn.'

'She means *very* good,' Eva whispered, with a wink. 'Have you ever used osha before?'

Vesta shook her head as she took the little packet of crushed brown substance.

'It helps if you talk to it,' Eva said. 'Ask it – *politely, Vesta* – to help us ward this place from demons that might try to come through.'

Vesta gave the packet a sceptical look, but nodded.

The rest of the herbs were less high-maintenance. Coralie was tasked to draw a wide circle around the opening with a chunk of resin from a copal tree, while Minerva scattered ground Angelica root and Henrietta gingerly laid down a carpet of scattered blue-green rue underneath the swirling pinprick. Francine carefully burned a sprig of mistletoe, and I picked apart a bunch of viciously sharp holly leaves, handing them out so each of us had a sprig tucked behind one ear.

Dear Maisie, I thought, mentally composing an email to my best friend who I'd left behind in London. *GREAT weekend in Paris with my new friends. Dancing, decapitating horrors from beyond, pagan warding rituals – you know, just girly things.*

'Please help us ward this place,' said Vesta to the osha in her hand as she scattered it across the concrete. 'We don't really know what we're doing, so we seriously need all the help we can get. You down? OK, great.'

She looked up and caught me grinning, and rolled her eyes.

'Are we ready?' Eva asked. We all nodded. 'Isobel,' Eva prompted, and she looked up. 'Ready?'

Isobel paused. She looked out at the Seine, and then up at the sky, where a few glittering stars were shining down through the city's air pollution. 'Ready,' she said.

We formed into our six-pointed star, and I gasped as the air between us began to glow with an eerie, dancing light – the scattered osha and rue and Angelica rising from the ground and starting to shine, filling the air with shimmering gold and silver specks.

Isobel began to chant words I didn't understand, in a language I could barely even identify – it could've been Gaelic, but it certainly wasn't any of the few words I had picked up. The demon portal began to glow too, a red spot in the air, like an infected wound in the skin of reality. It grew and pulsated, as if it was fighting back against our attempt to close it, until it was the size of a penny, and then a tennis ball. I could see the demon world now, and I felt slightly dizzy, remembering the pain as I started to see the jutting, strange shapes on the red horizon.

Was something wrong? Isobel was still chanting, her

voice cracked but strong. I swallowed and glanced at Eva, my hand itching to draw the long dagger I'd hidden up my sleeve – but she didn't look worried. She just looked . . . sad.

She looked *so* sad. She was standing within our double triangle, her black hair stirring lightly around her face as the herbs lifted and swirled, and her hands were clasped together in front of her heart, the knuckles white. Her lip trembled.

Isobel stopped chanting. She stared at the demon portal. She didn't look around as she spoke in a clear and quiet voice, the swirling lights settling in her white hair.

'This work I take for myself. This fate I weave with my own hands. So it is, and so it must be. There is nothing left to say. I love you all,' said Isobel. She closed her eyes. 'Goodbye.'

By the time my brain had caught up with my ears, she had stepped forward and plunged her hand into the portal.

I heard her scream, very briefly, and then she was gone.

'What?' gasped Minerva.

'What's happening?' said Vesta. 'Where did she go?'

Eva stood back, and said nothing.

'Where did she – no, she couldn't have – she's coming back, isn't she?' I demanded, though I knew the answer.

I love you all.

Goodbye.

'No!' Minerva screamed. 'Isobel!' She started forwards, breaking the line.

There was a flash of red light from the portal, and it winked out of existence.

The lights died. The air was full of drifting, settling dust. I felt like I couldn't breathe.

'Oh my God,' Vesta said, her voice hollow. She sank to her knees where she'd stood, tears gleaming in her eyes. 'She's ... *gone.*'

'No. No, I don't believe it.' Minerva strode over to Eva and struck her in the chest with a weak fist. 'Bring her back. Right now. Bring her *back!*'

'I am ... so sorry.' Eva choked. There were tears spilling down her cheeks too, but she stood there and took Minerva's punches. She reached up and tried to hold Minerva's shoulders, but Minerva shoved her aside. 'There was no other way.'

The Paris Trinity had huddled together and were staring at us, and at Eva, their faces drawn with shock.

'Eva, how could you?' Francine muttered. 'How could you do this?'

'There was – listen to me, Minerva, Vesta, there was *no other way.*'

Vesta let out a roar and rushed at Eva. She picked her up by her stab vest and dangled her over the glittering waters of the Seine. 'No other way?' she snarled. '*You* could have gone! Or – or *I* could! Not Isobel!'

Eva tried to speak, but she seemed too choked with fear and grief. After a long moment, Vesta threw her down on the concrete path. Eva struggled to her feet.

'Tell us. Tell us now. What happened?' I said, through gritted teeth. I hoped that the *or I will cut your head off* was implied.

'A puncture like that in the fabric of the world, it can

never be healed from our side,' Eva said. 'Someone must go through to close it, and if they do it right ...'

'They can never come back,' I said. 'She's ... she's trapped. In that *awful place*, with all those *demons* ...!'

'Isobel made this decision the moment she realised that this was a demon portal,' Eva said quickly. 'She wouldn't have sacrificed any of you – an active Trinity, and her *family*? No. I told her I would go, I begged her, but she said *no*, she had made up her mind.'

'How ... how could she do this to us? She barely even said goodbye!' Minerva said, and crumpled to the path, sobbing.

Eva got to her feet and reached into the vest. I watched her with furious curiosity – what was she doing *now*?

She pulled out three envelopes, and held them in front of her. 'She can explain this better than I can. She left you these—'

Vesta snatched the one with her name on it out of Eva's hand, crumpling it between her fingers, then turned and marched away.

'Where are you going?' Coralie asked, sounding like a lost child.

'Back to Eva's. I'm calling a cab. Come if you want,' Vesta said, without looking back. Coralie hurried after her.

Minerva shook her head when Eva tried to give her a letter, but I stepped forward and took mine gingerly, as if it might explode.

'I'll see you at yours too, Eva,' I muttered.

But I didn't want to go with Vesta. Not right now.

170

I pocketed the letter and then turned my back on the Trinities and Eva and the scattered herbs and the fading magic. I walked away down the river path, and let the cold air off the glittering Seine dry my tears.

CHAPTER TWELVE

I walked along the Seine for a long time, and then I crossed over a bridge and doubled back on myself along the other side of the river. I started to get tired, but I couldn't go back to Eva, not yet.

Not until I'd read Isobel's letter.

At last, as the winter darkness started to soften with hints that sunrise was on its way, and the city began to come alive, I wandered into the courtyard of the Louvre. It was so beautiful there, the old, pale brick glowing with the yellow lights shining from every window and archway, the gleaming glass pyramid in its wide, rippling fountain sending reflections of reflections bouncing back and forth.

I sat down on the low wall around the edge of the fountain, with my back to the pyramid, and opened the letter.

It said:

Dear Diana,

Please forgive me. I could not bear the debate that letting you all in on my decision in advance would have brought. I know you would have tried to talk me out of this, but my mind was made up and could not have been changed. I hope you can take some comfort from knowing this.

And please, do not grieve for me, because I will not die.

To be more specific: I may be killed. The demon world is very dangerous, and I am only one woman. But I will not simply die. Old age will not catch me, or disease. I will eventually end my life doing what I was born to do: killing demons. I have no wish to go quietly, and after spending more than half of my long life confined, seeking and training others, I relish the thought of fighting until my very last breath for the world that has allowed me to live in it so long.

There are a few things I should tell you.

First, I need you to look after the twins.

Vesta is strong in mind as well as body. In my day she would probably have been called a harridan, and I smile to think she would have worn the label with pride. But pride may be her downfall - I fear she may be brittle, unable to handle failure, her own or other people's.

Minerva bears her strength lightly and is more flexible, in some ways more grown-up than her sister. But I don't want her serious nature to become a crutch for others in the years to come. If she takes on too much responsibility, she will come to resent it. I want her to live a full and happy life.

(Of course, I have written something similar to them about you. If you wish to compare notes, on your own head be it.)

Secondly: the Demon Hunter line must continue. I understand that none of you want to think about children at your age – you grow up so much more slowly these days, and that's no bad thing. But you must think about it.

Lastly, and most importantly: it has been a privilege to meet you, and to train you. In a long life of fighting demons and training Trinities, you three are my triumph. A lot of that is down to you, Diana. In a very short time, I've grown to admire and love your strength, your kindness, even your sense of humour.

I don't know who will come to look after you. Eva will reach out, but there aren't too many 'spare' Demon Hunters these days. I wish I'd had time to choose my own replacement, to make sure that they were up to standard. Whoever it is, respect them, but do not let them hold you back.

Being a Seer can be a blessing and a curse. Do not be afraid to ask Eva for help. Start a diary.

I think that's all – I could write forever, and it wouldn't be enough, so I will stop here.

All my love and respect, forever.
Isobel

'Er – *ça va*, love?' said a voice. I looked up into the kindly, blurry face of a middle-aged lady holding a camera.

'I'm – I'm—' I said, but my throat closed around the word 'OK'.

'Oh, you're an American? Here,' said the lady, whose accent was one of the cluster I sucked at identifying, from the north of England. 'Have a tissue, duck. Can I call someone for you?'

I dabbed at my eyes and shook my head. Then I remembered that my phone had been through a portal and then taken a dip in the Seine with me.

'Can I . . . can I use your phone to call a cab?'

'Of course, dear,' said the lady.

I couldn't take it. The kindness pushed me over the edge. I laid my head on the shoulder of a total stranger and sobbed.

I arrived back at Eva's place just as the sun was coming up over the tops of the apartment buildings, cold light casting harsh black shadows as it slanted down the steep Montmartre streets.

Even with Eva and the Paris Trinity milling about making coffee and speaking French in hushed voices, the place felt . . . *empty*. The minimalist decorations suddenly felt cold, hard, almost like they were mocking me, telling me that there was no comfort here. That we weren't welcome. I knew I was reading too much into it, but I couldn't seem to stop. I felt like the place was *watching* me.

It was time to go home. There was nothing more for us here, and Sebastian probably needed us. I accepted a cup of coffee without speaking, and tried and failed not to think about Isobel's house.

I called my dad, and cried some more. Then I found Minerva standing on Eva's balcony, and I hugged her for a long time.

'Where's V?' I asked.

'She's going to be OK,' Minerva said, which wasn't quite the question I'd asked, but maybe it was what I'd meant. Eventually Minerva seemed to catch up with reality, and she wiped her eyes. 'I think she's on the phone to Seb. I didn't want to ...'

'Oh, God. Yeah, right.' I let out a long breath and drew out my letter.

I thought about the letter I'd found after Mom died – I kept it close to me for five years, before Edinburgh, before the Trinity – the one that the twins' mother had written to mine, years ago, telling her that they forgave her for running away.

And now, I had this one from Isobel.

She hadn't mentioned Mom at all.

I stared over the road at the windows on the opposite apartment building and imagined the shutters slamming closed one by one, blocking out the light.

How could she? How could she write me a beautiful, touching letter and not think to tell me that she forgave Kara for leaving?

Unless ... she never did forgive her. Unless after all these years it was still too raw to talk about. Unless she thought I wouldn't want to hear that she thought my mom was selfish and a traitor ...

I could've taken it, if she'd ever said it to my face. I could have told her everything Mom did that proved she was neither. Finally, in some way, I would have been able to fight my mom's corner for her. And I would have won.

'Do you want to know what she said about you?' Minerva asked, jolting me out of my thoughts, and just in time – this wasn't the moment to take issue with Isobel's final words, not when she was *gone*, and her absence still felt like the ache in my muscles after a hard day's training.

'Hah! Er, no,' I said. 'I don't think I do. Not right now, anyway. You?'

'Go on.'

I thought about Isobel's message, and weirdly, began to smile. The expression felt very alien on my face. 'She says you need to have more fun,' I told Minerva. 'Basically. She says don't ... don't forget to have a life.'

'Oh my God,' said Minerva, leaning over the rail and looking down at the street. 'My dead great-aunt wants me to get a life. That is ... fair, actually.'

'Girls,' said a gentle voice behind us. 'I think it's time. When you're ready, you all need to go home to your families.'

It was Eva. She seemed nervous, and I felt a stab of guilt.

'I'm sorry we all blew up at you last night,' I said. 'I know it wasn't your fault.'

Tears leaped to Eva's eyes, and she swiped them away with one elegant finger. 'Thank you, Diana. You know you will always be welcome in Paris. Here, I have written down all of our phone numbers and emails. Call any time, or Skype, if you want to talk about anything.'

I took the folded piece of paper and held it tight to my heart for a moment.

Henrietta, Coralie and Francine came to the alley to see us off. There was a lot of cheek-kissing.

'You *have* to come back,' Henrietta said. 'In the summer, or before then.'

'Come for Christmas!' Coralie grinned. 'Christmas here, it is *magical*.'

'Maybe *you* should come to us for Christmas,' said Vesta, cracking the first smile I'd seen from her all day. 'It's Scotland. There will be snow. The castle looks like Hogwarts, and we can make the most epic snowman ever.'

We got into formation around the place where the tear in reality was, but I stepped aside and turned to Eva.

'Wait, Eva – how do you make a portal? Can we do it ourselves, if we want to come back, or go somewhere else?'

'Oh, it is actually very simple,' said Eva. 'You need another Demon Hunter on the other end to make a connection, but they don't have to be in a Trinity – as you see. And any portal you open should stay open, at least for a few weeks. I will email you the instructions.'

'Thank you,' I said, and stepped into formation. There was that sound again, the sensation of rushing wind, and then I felt myself stumble and fall on my butt in the wet grass.

We were home.

'It feels wrong,' said Vesta.

Sebastian, Minerva and I nodded sadly. They had all

come to my house, and we'd holed up in one of the many impeccably-decorated and never-used bedrooms on the second floor. For once, I was glad that Dad had been so carried away when he'd bought this place. Maybe fate had found a way, like Eva said – perhaps one day all these rooms would come in handy.

I thought of Isobel's injunction to think about the next generation, and smiled to myself, imagining a huge clan of Demon Hunter babies filling the house with screaming laughter, powers going off in every room.

I wasn't sure I wanted to personally *have* all those babies, but suddenly it seemed like a future I could imagine being part of.

Dad had hugged me tight as soon as we'd come in, and called Isobel a 'fierce old broad', which made me smile, because I could imagine the look on her face if she'd heard him. Then he'd wandered off to order pizza for all of us, even though it was barely midday.

Vesta and Minerva were on the bed, and Sebastian and I were sitting on the floor, leaning against the mattress.

'It is wrong. I mean . . . she was four hundred years old,' said Sebastian. 'But I thought when she went we would have some warning . . . '

'No – I mean yes,' Vesta said, reaching down and running her hand through Sebastian's hair – such a thoughtlessly intimate gesture that I wondered if I ought to be looking. Sebastian flushed bright red. 'But I mean, just . . . just going on with our lives. I don't want to do that. People get *funerals*. That's what funerals are for, they're for . . . ' she trailed off.

'For saying goodbye,' said Minerva, her voice high-pitched with the effort of keeping it together. She swallowed. 'But there's no body to bury. Isobel is just ... gone.'

'Then, let's say goodbye some other way,' I said, sitting up. 'Let's ..... let's take some of her things up to Arthur's Seat and bury them there.'

'That's a great idea,' said Minerva, her voice still choked. 'Let's do it tonight.'

Sebastian nodded slowly. 'Yes. We should send her off, and then we can ... we can move on,' he said.

The pizza arrived. We were all incredibly glad.

None of us really wanted to go back to Isobel's house. For me, the memory of all those visions I'd had of her living there over the years gave it a special horror, beyond the idea of looking her taxidermied animals in the eye and feeling the chill in the kitchen because she'd never got back to set the fire in the Aga. I had witnessed how indelibly her soul was bound up in the bricks of that house, and now, to begin dismantling that life ... the whole thing seemed far too big to deal with, but far too important not to.

But we weren't expecting to pull up in Ruby to find lights on behind the heavy curtains.

We stood out on the street and stared at the glow in the windows for a long few minutes. Nothing moved, but the house looked ... *occupied*. I tried, and failed, not to let my imagination run wild. What if we opened the door and found Isobel there waiting for us, smiling, telling us it was all a huge mistake ...

'Burglars,' said Vesta, coming to a very different conclusion and clenching her fists tight. 'I'm going to *kill* them.' She stomped up the steps and thrust the front door open. It wasn't locked. The rest of us followed behind her, fists at the ready, but Vesta got there first. She threw open the door to the living room and yelled, 'Get out! Get out of this house! What are you doing here?'

Peering around her shoulders, I didn't see the gang of young men I'd been expecting. Instead, a single middle-aged Chinese man with a streak of grey in his black hair was standing in the middle of the room. He was holding a box that said *BOOKS*.

This did not seem like burglar behaviour to me.

'Ah – hello, you must be Vesta,' he said, and I almost reeled at the familiarity of his accent – it was Californian, and not just CA; he had to be from San Francisco or somewhere nearby. 'And this must be Minerva, obviously, and are you Diana?'

'Who are you?' Minerva said. 'And why are you packing up Isobel's things?'

'Oh, I'm not,' said the man. 'I left that for you. These are my things.'

We stared at him. I slowly started to take in the other changes around the room – lots of the taxidermy had been moved against the wall, and the surfaces that they'd sat on now held more cardboard boxes.

'Isobel's been gone less than twenty-four hours,' I said. 'And you're ... *moving in*?'

'She and Eva put out the call to the Demon Hunter

181

families a little before she ... went away,' the man said. 'And I happened to be living in London, so I just took the first flight up. I'm truly sorry that we had to meet like this – but it's a pleasure to meet you all. My name is John Yao, and I'll be training you from now on.'

'A ... pleasure,' said Vesta under her breath. 'Is it?'

'You can't just move in,' Minerva said. 'I mean, it's good that they could find someone,' she added, making an obvious effort to be reasonable, 'but you can't do this. This isn't your house!'

'Well, that's interesting actually; you see, technically it is. Another reason I was ideal to come and do the job. When the house was first built, Isobel bought it with money borrowed from my family. We go back a very, very long way, you know; by the seventeenth century we had trade routes all over Europe and Asia – well, you don't care about that. We had money, and Isobel had none. She never repaid the loan – obviously, she didn't have to, it was an agreement between Demon Hunters – but now that she's gone, the house and all its contents belongs to my family. I'm here to look after it, as well as you.'

He looked around with a smug smile on his face, giving the building an appraising look that I didn't like one bit.

Who *was* this man, with his epic family history and his money and his entitled, cheery manner? Would he want to strip out everything about the house that had made it Isobel's, that had made it *home* to so many generations of Demon Hunters? Or maybe even tear it down?

Didn't he know that, for all intents and purposes, our grandmother had just died?

'We're here to take some of Isobel's things,' Sebastian said.

John Yao smiled benevolently. I hated him.

'Of course, feel free, they are her things. Please, not the old Demon Hunter artefacts, though. Those belong to the community, and we may need them.'

I felt Vesta draw herself up beside me, and I took her elbow, afraid that if she kicked off she would tear down half the house all by herself. 'Fine,' I said. 'Come on, let's go downstairs.'

I led Vesta through the sitting room and into the kitchen, towards the basement stairs.

'What are you doing? Don't you want to tell him off?' she hissed.

'No,' I whispered back. 'I want to get my hands on Isobel's artefacts before he does.'

CHAPTER THIRTEEN

'Is it supposed to be doing that?' I said, gazing up at the sky as we began to scale the final rocky approach to the summit of Arthur's Seat. The others all turned to look, and I heard their intakes of breath in the still darkness.

The moon was red. Not just the orangey-red of a harvest moon, but a serious, deep, dark red.

'Oh, it's a blood moon,' murmured Sebastian. 'I knew there was one due this week, but I just ... forgot ... ' he trailed off. I stared at the red moon rising over Arthur's Seat and I felt a kind of tug on my heart, something I couldn't quite explain away as grief or tiredness or anger.

We had brought a few of Isobel's things. The salt and pepper shaker mice from the kitchen table. Her sword, and the book where her story had been told: the confession, burning, and misreported death of Isobel Gowdie, witch.

The ground was too tough up on the Seat for us to bury the things there, so we found a small hollow lower down the slope and piled rocks on top of them so they wouldn't be found and disturbed. Then we went on up to the summit.

I felt strangely light, as if I had left everything I didn't need behind in that hollow. My grief, my anger, my pain, my imagination's vivid suggestions about what might be happening to Isobel right now ...

Even Mom. Not her memory or her love, of course, but perhaps I could leave behind the need to know that she was forgiven.

In a way, I didn't *want* Isobel's true forgiveness, I just wanted her to *tell* me Kara was forgiven. That wasn't fair.

Mom had been who she'd been, and if Isobel hadn't forgiven her, hadn't known the true Kara Fleming ... that was sad for Isobel, but I didn't need to let it weigh me down.

All I had with me, all I needed, was my family and my self. I felt like I could reach the top of the hills and carry on walking, walk right up to the moon.

We did stop at the summit, though. Sebastian sat down on a rock, and the Trinity got into formation, moving slowly. The power, when it came, was ... strange. It wasn't like the fizzing energy I normally felt; it was softer, deeper. It tugged at me. The same as the moon had done, I realised.

As one, although we hadn't planned it, all three of us sat down on the spot, still connected. I saw Minerva close her eyes and turn her face to the moon. Vesta reached down beside her, and her fingers roamed the stony ground, digging underneath a handful of rocks, discovering, connecting. I looked neither up nor down – I looked at the twins, and at Sebastian.

I thought about Isobel. I thought about her taxidermy and her old-lady jumpers and her intense, back-breaking training routines. I thought about what it must be like to hang your whole life, literally your continued existence, on the life of your worst enemy. And then not to bring him down yourself – to raise the children of your children's children's children until one day you get lucky ... and you know that your time is almost at an end.

'Isobel,' I said. I was surprised that I'd said it aloud.

'You are loved,' whispered Minerva, without opening her eyes.

'You are missed,' said Vesta.

And then all three of us, together, spoke a word: 'Goodbye.'

And ... that was it. I knew it, somehow, and I shifted so that we weren't sitting in formation any more.

I looked over at Sebastian. He was crying silently, hands folded between his knees.

I got up and went to sit beside him on his rock, and wrapped my arms around him. I hoped that I could give him some of the lightness I still felt. He leaned his head against mine. Then I felt another pair of arms overlapping mine as Minerva sat down on the other side of him and rested her cheek on his shoulder. Vesta joined us, kneeling in front of him and putting her arms around his shoulders. They pressed their heads together.

'Well, this is nice,' Sebastian said. 'I should cry more often if it means getting hugged like this.'

'I think this is a one-off, buddy,' said Minerva.

Vesta simply made a *mm* noise.

Then Sebastian's phone vibrated in his pocket. He disentangled himself from our limbs enough to get it out and look at the message. He sighed.

'How do you all feel?' he said.

'I felt all right until you said that,' I said, smiling at him. 'Why?'

'Because there's something that happened that I haven't told you about yet. It just didn't seem like the time. But if we're going to deal with it, we might need to do it soon.'

As one, all three of us girls pulled away. The lightness was leaving me, but that was OK. Not everything could be taken lightly.

Sebastian tapped out and sent a text message before he spoke again.

'We caught James Armstrong in the act,' he said. 'He was going to get a bunch of his classmates to make a blood sacrifice – then one of them tried to back out, and he nearly persuaded them to kill him. They're all locked up now, I think,' he added hurriedly. 'In the medical ward at the school. The staff are trying to hush it up, but we definitely think the boys are trying to raise a demon. In fact . . . we're pretty sure it's Oriax.'

'Wait a second,' I frowned. 'Who exactly is this *we*?'

187

For a second, I had a horrible vision of Sebastian and Dad roaming the halls of Wallington School together.

Then I heard footsteps climbing the rocky slope, and a voice said, 'I am.'

I knew that voice. Even from just those two syllables.

I got to my feet and stared, my heart in my mouth, as Alex crested the hill.

'*You*,' Vesta snarled. 'Stay back, demon.'

But in my peripheral vision, I caught sight of Sebastian taking her hands in his and shaking his head. 'It's OK. He's safe,' he said.

'Are you *sure*?' Minerva muttered.

'As sure as it's possible to be,' Sebastian said. 'Which, to be fair, is not very sure. I think if he was going to kill me he'd have done it already, if that helps.'

Alex stopped a healthy distance from us. In the strange, red moonlight he looked every bit the movie star I'd thought he should be when we first met.

'Hello, Diana,' he said.

I didn't reply. I couldn't. No words were finding their way from my brain to my lips.

'I – I know that apologising can never make any of what I did right,' he said. 'I know that you don't necessarily trust me, and that's OK. I don't need you to. But right now I need your help. Again,' he added, with a little head-tilt and a sheepish smile.

'Of course,' I said, words now apparently bypassing my brain altogether. 'Of course we'll help you.'

'Will we, though?' Minerva muttered.

'Yes,' said Sebastian and Vesta together.

'Believe me, you're going to want to look into this,' Alex said. 'Some of the things we heard in the school were ... familiar.'

A chill settled at the base of my spine. 'Come on, then,' I said. 'Pull up a rock. Tell us everything.'

Between them, Seb and Alex filled us in on everything they'd seen and heard going down at Wallington School. The creeping feeling in my spine didn't go away, it only spread up my back and across my neck.

'Are you sure it is Oriax?' asked Vesta.

'I'm sure,' muttered Alex. He blinked twice, slowly, as if he was trying to clear an after-image from his vision. 'But, either way, it's definitely demonic and you three are the only ones who can stop it.'

He looked at me, and I thought I saw him smile, but then he looked away and I wondered if I'd imagined it.

'How are we going to get in, though? Unless you've got three more gardening uniforms ...'

'No, definitely not. Three young, pretty female groundskeepers would definitely attract comment.'

Again ... was that a glance at me? Or ... or was he just having a conversation, making occasional eye contact, like a normal person?

Don't freak out, Di, I told myself. *Get a grip. Just ... don't go there. Not right now.*

'No, there's actually a much better way in for you, if you come tomorrow night. It's the school's Benefactors' Dinner – a bunch of old rich alumni getting wined and dined as a reward for donating money to the school, as far as I can tell from chatting to the janitors.'

'Hang on,' Sebastian frowned. 'You're telling me they've been on total lockdown dealing with a demon infestation and a bunch of psychotic Year Nines hopped up on blood sacrifices, but they're going ahead with the fancy schmancy fundraising party?'

Alex shrugged. 'Don't ask me. Maybe they think they can use the money to hire a fleet of therapists, or demon-proof the swimming pool. Either way, it's a good thing. I can get you three in with the catering staff, then you can find Oriax and destroy it.'

He definitely looked at me, that time, but this wasn't flirting. It was pleading. *Please. Tell me you can destroy him.*

I thought of everything Oriax and Kincaid had made Alex do, and everything I still didn't know about what had happened to him.

'We will,' I said. 'I promise.'

'Well, then we're doing this,' said Vesta. She sighed. 'One other thing though, and I can't quite believe that I'm saying this, but ... should we tell Yao what we're doing?'

'No,' said Minerva firmly. 'We can take care of ourselves.'

I definitely, completely agreed.

I also really *hoped* we were both right.

CHAPTER FOURTEEN

'... and the dessert is Flavours of Blackcurrant – blackcurrant meringue and a blackcurrant foam with charcoal smoke and salted cream,' the head caterer was saying. She was a stern-looking woman who, in a previous life, had definitely been either a duchess or a housekeeper. Or possibly a drill sergeant. I hadn't quite decided which.

The three of us nodded solemnly, and Minerva even took notes as the caterer described to the gaggle of waitresses the speed at which we would need to serve Flavours of Blackcurrant to the old rich men in the great hall next door, so that the blackcurrant foam wouldn't turn into blackcurrant slime. I noted that all the waiting staff were young women, and I wondered if it was chance or if some old perv had expressed a preference. Either way, it didn't feel remotely surprising that the only way the three of us could get into Wallington School was to essentially dress as servants.

'Mobile phones,' said the head caterer, holding out a clear plastic bag.

'What are you going to do, *sous-vide* them?' Vesta asked, holding on tight to her brand new phone.

'I'm going to lock them away,' sneered the caterer. 'So that spoiled little millennial brats like you don't get bored halfway through service and decide to play a couple of rounds of *Choco Crush* when you should be working.' She snatched the phone from Vesta's hands and Vesta glared at her. 'And one more word of cheek like that out of you, and you're fired. Understand?'

'Yes, ma'am,' said Vesta. I could *feel* her suppressing the urge to snap a salute. The caterer seemed to consider whether or not this constituted cheek, then turned and walked off with her bag full of phones.

'They're ready for us. The speech is kicking off in a minute,' said a young man in a purple waistcoat, sticking his head around the door to the kitchen.

The head caterer clapped her hands together. 'Service!' she yelled. 'Two hundred pheasant, and no slouching!'

The chefs had already been fussing away at the details like nervous automatons, probably for hours and hours before we arrived, but now the kitchen leaped into a higher gear and very soon there were six dishes out on the counter and we grabbed two each and walked into the hall.

It was just as grand as I'd been expecting, with wood-panelled walls, polished floors and vaulted ceilings.

Perhaps another time I would have been impressed. Right now, I just felt stifled. Nobody but us and a few members of the kitchen staff had any idea that this place had been as quiet as a tomb for days, and its presumably-boisterous students – not that I had ever seen a single one except Armstrong – had been grounded. Its precious reputation for academic rigour and hooliganism had been put on hold while a handful of boys tried to spill enough blood to summon a demon.

Just how much blood was that, anyway?

Here in this hall, old men in suits and academic gowns chatted with each other, and with coiffed and expensively-perfumed middle-aged women, and not one of them thought there was anything strange going on.

I had no intention of waitressing an entire five-course dinner for two hundred people. But we had to pick the right moment to vanish – ideally some time that would not mean our fellow waitresses got it in the neck, so not right before or during service for the first course.

As we were handing out plates, and I was trying to remember the rules of waitressing that I'd swiftly googled on the way here, a genial-looking round-faced old man who I thought might be the headmaster walked up to the podium and coughed politely.

'Before I begin the long round of thank-yous,' he said, 'I must make some apologies. First, from Sir Bryan Joyce, who couldn't be here tonight, and secondly from myself, for appearing in *unsuitable attire*, as we say to the boys.'

There were sniggers from around the hall, and I glanced up at what the Head was wearing. It was a suit. It looked like a nice suit, much like all the other nice suits sitting around me. So what . . .

'Unfortunately, my official robes suffered a bit of an accident – a freak infestation of moths. So I suppose you could say that my plans for dressing up this evening have been . . . *mothballed*.'

There was polite applause, which is how I realised it was meant to be a joke.

I turned and spotted Minerva and Vesta. They had both frozen in place too, and they were staring at me.

Moths.

It was true, then. Alex was right.

Oriax was here.

We regrouped in the kitchen, hiding from our duties by looking like we were doing the washing-up.

'Listen,' I whispered to the others. 'Oriax is here, influencing the kids. But it can't be possessing them yet. When I saw Kincaid making his deal with it, even before he gave it his own life, he was trying to make a sacrifice. A baby. I think that Oriax needs a death to possess one of them. That means we can still catch it on the back foot, while it's in his true form and it's vulnerable. I hope,' I added.

I wished, suddenly and fiercely, that Isobel was here.

Perhaps we ought to have told John Yao what we were doing. But as soon as the thought occurred to me, I put it out of my head again. We'd made that choice, and we were going to have to deal with it, whatever the consequences.

'Let's get to this medical wing Sebastian was talking about, then,' said Minerva. 'If the boys are still there, we can talk to them – maybe even use them to draw Oriax out somewhere far away from all these people.'

'Demon-summoning field trip-slash-kidnapping,' grinned Vesta. 'I like it.'

We slipped out and headed for the exit to the front hall of the school. But the massive double doors were shut now.

Well, it might be a little unsubtle, but we had to get out of there. I pushed on the door. It rattled slightly, but it didn't open.

'V, the door's stuck,' I muttered. 'Give me a hand.'

Vesta rolled her eyes, stepped to my side, and tugged on the door. She pulled, then she pushed, then she looked at me with a frown that I did not like at all, not one bit.

'It's locked,' she said. 'It's been bolted. From the outside. I can get it open, but not, y'know, subtly.'

I looked around at the hundreds of people eating their posh dinners, and my heart sank.

'Maybe it's ... a mistake. A policy. Insurance,' I babbled. 'Maybe it's fine. C'mon, let's go out the back.'

Leaving via the kitchen door meant passing the head caterer, but she was busy bullying the chefs who were dealing with the soup course, so that wasn't much of a problem.

What was a problem was the fact that this door, too, was locked.

'We're shut in,' I whispered to Vesta. 'Someone's locked all of these people in here ...'

'How powerful do you reckon you'd be,' Vesta replied, her voice dripping with fake casualness, 'if you sacrificed about two hundred and fifty people to a demon?'

I reached into my pocket for my new phone, to call Sebastian and Alex and have them come and get us – all of us – out of this. Then I remembered – my phone was in a plastic bag, somewhere in the kitchen, and I couldn't see where.

'Want me to bust us out of here?' Vesta asked.

'Yes please,' Minerva and I chorused. 'We can't cause a panic,' I pointed out. 'It'll only force the boys' hands if they're planning something.'

'They're only what, fourteen?' Vesta muttered, putting her hands to the doorframe, testing the wood and metal with little prods. 'What are they going to do? March in here with a bunch of chainsaws and hack us all to death?'

'I bet there's a couple of guns somewhere,' Minerva said. 'After all, this is a posh school; they probably go hunting their own deer or something.'

I didn't like that thought, but I didn't quite believe it either. The kind of guns she was talking about would be far too clumsy and slow to take out this many people – and once the doors were open, people would start to escape.

No, there was something else happening here. I just wasn't sure yet what it was.

Vesta placed her hand carefully on the door and gave it a hard shove. There was the sound of something on the other side of it pinging off and skittering away across the concrete, and then the door swung open.

We slipped quietly out into the back car park. Ruby was hard to miss – her distinctive Mini shape and peeling cherry-red paint stood out, especially among all the big, gleaming black cars that filled the car park right now. We made a beeline for her, but after a couple of steps, Minerva swore.

'They're not there.'

Sebastian and Alex were supposed to be waiting for us out here, in case anything happened inside. Well, anything had definitely happened – so where were they?

'Seb!' Vesta called out, as if he might just be hiding behind one of the Rolls-Royces and waiting for his cue to jump out at her. There was no reply.

'Alex?' I hissed. 'Are you there?'

Nothing.

I cracked my knuckles and put out my hand.

I hadn't taken a reading from anything since Paris. Since I'd touched the demon portal and got a face-full of pain.

I wasn't sure if Vesta or Minerva had noticed, but I had. At first it'd just been a hesitation about picking up unfamiliar objects, but this morning I'd found myself hesitating to touch my grip on my own bedroom door or pick up my own clothes.

I had to stop that, and now was a good a time.

I laid my hand gingerly on the surface of the door, where I imagined Sebastian would normally push it shut. I winced as I made contact – the car was freezing, and slightly damp.

I blinked.

Nothing around me changed, but I heard a voice behind me, and turned.

Sebastian and Alex were standing beside the car, hands in their pockets.

'Guys!' I said. 'Where have ... you ...'

But my voice came out as an almost-noiseless sigh, and when I looked around, I couldn't see Minerva or Vesta. This was a vision – it was just that it was happening exactly where I'd been standing. Everything seemed the same, from the position of the stars to the scattered leaves at my feet. The time must be only a couple of minutes before we arrived.

'... was really cool of you, man,' Alex muttered.

Sebastian shook his head. 'Just going on the evidence,' he said. 'Anyway, listen, if you hurt Di again, the twins will break your legs, so ... be careful there.'

'Why Di? No particular thing about Di,' Alex said, shrugging exaggeratedly.

My heart climbed up into my throat. Even in a vision, I could tell that he was lying, or rather, kind of adorably trying to.

Sebastian laughed at him. 'Right, no, you're not completely – what was that?'

No! I thought, selfishly. *Finish your sentence, Sebastian!*

But he didn't get the chance. A flash of something black swirled past me, and I twisted on the spot and saw Armstrong standing between two cars, a creepy smile on his face.

Seb and Alex both yelled, and when I turned back, teenage boys with ropes had climbed up over Ruby's bonnet and grabbed them.

I yanked my hand away. The boys all vanished and the twins came back into view.

'Armstrong and his gang have got them. They've

198

busted out of the medical ward somehow and now they're running around with ropes, grabbing people. Where would they have taken them?'

The twins both shrugged.

'All right. They couldn't go too far, because someone would notice them. But if they're keeping Seb and Alex prisoner they must have somewhere private.' I cast around and spotted a shed on the edge of the parking lot. 'Come on.'

As we drew closer, I held up my hand for stealth and the twins both muffled their footsteps and breathing, the way Isobel had taught us. Armstrong might still be inside, the boys might be holding hostages . . . I crept up to the door, and I heard voices. It was Alex and Seb, and they were . . .

Well, *gossiping.*

'Her. Really?' said Alex.

'Well, you needn't say it like that,' Sebastian's voice complained.

'I mean, no offence,' Alex said, and even from outside the door I could hear the grin in his tone. 'But . . . you're basically a tiny twig man. And you're into *Vesta*? Wouldn't she, like . . . crush you?'

'Oh, shut up and keep trying to reach the shears.'

I looked behind me and found Vesta right at my elbow. Had she heard that too?

Vesta moved me firmly aside, drew back her foot and kicked the door in. It hit the concrete floor with a *slam* and a cloud of dust. She crossed the small room to where Sebastian was sitting tied up with his back to Alex, knelt down and kissed him so hard the two boys' heads knocked together.

I guess she heard.

Minerva and I loitered awkwardly in the doorway for a few seconds before I said, 'V, the ropes?'

'Mmf,' she said, and broke off kissing Sebastian for long enough to go around the boys, snapping ropes with a small grunt of effort. Then she lifted Seb to his feet by the lapels of his cardigan and kissed him again.

'Diana,' said Alex, peeling himself out of the ropes, 'we've got trouble.'

'I know,' I said. 'They've locked the doors to the main hall. The whole banquet is a trap.'

'Ah. Well that's bad,' he said, massaging his wrists. 'Because after they dragged us in here, they left with half a dozen cans of petrol.'

CHAPTER FIFTEEN

'This was supposed to be fact-finding, and maybe a little light exorcism,' Minerva said. 'We didn't even bring our own weapons. How do we stop them *burning down the school*?'

Vesta produced a kitchen knife – from where, I couldn't have told you – and shrugged. 'I'm good to go.'

'I know where the rest of you can get some weapons,' Alex said. 'Aside from the kitchen. This is a posh school – there are state-of-the-art archery bows and fencing swords in the sports shed.'

'No shotguns?' I asked.

Alex shook his head. 'Not that I know of.'

'Shame.'

I looked up at him, and he met my gaze with a slightly strange expression ... a slow, uncertain smile. I remembered what Sebastian had said – what he'd been in the middle of saying – and flushed and turned away from Alex quickly.

'It's, um.' he cleared his throat. 'It's all under lock and key, of course, but . . .'

'Yeah, not going to be a problem,' said Vesta, and strode out of the shed with the carving knife in one hand and Sebastian's hand held tight in the other. He followed her with a dazed look on his face.

The main door to the school was ajar, and I crept up to it, the rapier I'd taken from the sports shed held loosely in one hand. We hadn't done a lot of training with rapiers, but I was banking hard on the fact that this one was sharp and pointy. Minerva already had an arrow notched to the string of a sleek blue bow – not quite the powerful hunting weapon she was used to, but at point-blank range an Olympic-grade sports bow would just have to do.

I smelled smoke and swore under my breath. Leaning in to peer through the door, I saw flames flickering up from a pile of fabric that might've been heavy curtains, and the shapes of several teenaged boys moving through the smoke, laying out ropes that dripped with greasy-looking fluid.

'We've got to get everyone out. Sebastian, call the fire department. Then run around the back, make sure they know the kitchen door's open and get them all out; tell them to run. At least the smoke ought to convince them this is serious.'

'Shouldn't this place have a sprinkler system?' Vesta said, peering into the gloom.

'It does,' Alex muttered. 'They must've turned it off. I can fix it.'

'Alex,' I said, turning and touching his arm.

It was warm and solid, and I completely forgot what I was going to say.

'Um. I, um. Good,' I eventually finished lamely. I patted his arm, as if he was a big friendly dog. *Good boy.* 'Go do that. And ... be careful.'

'I will,' Alex said. 'Diana, this is Oriax ... it's using these boys' worst instincts to get them to do his bidding. Last time we were here, there was a lot of talk of women remembering their place.' I saw Minerva bristle and Vesta's eyes narrow angrily. 'I know. Just, all three of you watch yourselves, OK? If they feel threatened, the boys'll hurt you any way they can.'

I nodded, hoping that he couldn't tell that my heart had just grown three sizes.

But also, maybe, not caring all *that* much if he could.

'Let's go,' he said to Sebastian. Sebastian moved to leave, and Vesta grabbed him and kissed him again.

'OK, now you can go,' she said.

I met Alex's eyes. Then we both looked away.

The boys ran off around the side of the building, and I stared after them for a second.

'All right,' said Minerva, rolling her eyes. 'Now that's out of the way, if you two could just stop being aggressively heterosexual for a second? The building is literally *on fire*.'

Crap. She was right. What was I doing?

'We've got to find you a girlfriend.' Vesta grinned, as I peered in through the door again, trying to come up with a strategy.

'I don't want a girlfriend who makes me forget that the floor's on fire!' Minerva retorted.

'Yeah, you do though,' said Vesta.

'We'll try to creep up on them, use the smoke as cover,' I said. 'Take them down and separate them from each other. And from the fire. You guys ready?'

'As I'll ever be,' said Minerva, pulling her shirt up over her nose and mouth. Vesta and I copied her, and then I forced myself to step up to the door and slip inside.

The reception hall was filled with smoke. I kept low, trying to breathe gently through my shirt so as not to cough and give us away within ten seconds. The flames had spread from the pile of curtains to a line of gas-soaked rope at the base of the doors to the great hall, but more ropes, still-unlit, were draped over the receptionist's desk and up the long flight of stairs.

We crept along the side of the room, until I spotted a pair of feet in blue slippers pass by. I lunged, and dragged the boy's legs out from under him. Minerva swooped at the same time and slapped her hand over the mask he was wearing across his mouth. He didn't have time to shout – he just stared up at us in confusion and anger.

'Mmm-mmmmmmph!' He was trying to cry out. I pulled off one of his slippers and stuffed it deep inside his mouth under the mask, so he couldn't spit it out.

'Be quiet, and we won't have to knock you unconscious,' Vesta told him.

'V, get him out,' I muttered. 'Out of the way.'

Vesta nodded, threw the gagged boy over her shoulder and ran for the doors.

I tried and failed not to think *and then there were two.*

'Who's there?' called a muffled voice.

'Mitchell's gone,' said another.

'Where's Armstrong?' said a third, also muffled. They all must be wearing masks.

'Light the fires. Don't stop.' That was James's voice. Except it was ... not quite the way I remembered it from our meeting on the street. It was deeper, and there was a strange tone to it. It sounded a little as if, at the same time as James had spoken, someone a very long way away had struck a metal sheet with a large hammer.

That was probably a bad sign.

'They're here!' one of the boys yelled, and I looked up to see two of them rushing at me. One was carrying a hockey stick, and the other had a rapier like mine. I stood up and parried his thrust in a single movement.

'Give up, now!' I yelled, as Minerva leaped from the smoke around my feet and grabbed the hockey stick before it could smack me in the side of the head. 'You don't want to do this!'

'Your victims have—' Minerva broke off, choking, and the boy with the hockey stick wrenched it out of her hands and aimed a hard swing at her stomach. She danced back, just in time.

'They've gone!' I shouted, parrying another stab. 'You won't raise Oriax this way. You've *lost.*'

The boy with the rapier hesitated, then turned and

ran into the smoke. I had a brief pang of guilt – what if he burned himself, what if he choked? But then the one with the hockey stick swung it again and I ducked and stabbed my rapier into the top of his foot, piercing through his shoe and into the flesh. The boy screamed and tumbled over, dropping the stick, which Minerva picked up.

'How many more are there?' Minerva choked.

'At least two. Maybe more. Get him outside,' I said. Minerva leaned down and dragged the still-screaming boy towards the door by the collar of his coat.

Apart from the crackling of the fire, everything went very quiet in the hall.

'How dare they?' cried a voice, and I spun around, one arm covering my nose and mouth, slashing at the smoke with my rapier. I could see nothing, not even the floor. My eyes were stinging. I had to get out of here . . .

'How dare they think they can challenge us?' said the voice again. Now it sounded like it was behind me. I lashed out, cutting the smoke in two, but it reformed and flowed over my head once more.

My lungs were burning. I *had to get out*. I headed for the door, or where I thought the door was . . . and silhouetted in the light from outside, I saw two figures. I stumbled towards them, not able to care that they were waiting for me. Their faces became clearer as I got closer to the fresh air: it was Armstrong, and another boy, an Indian kid in a Superman T-shirt.

Perhaps the most ironic T-shirt choice of all time.

They stood side by side. The Indian boy was shaking

and panting through his mask, but Armstrong barely seemed to be breathing.

'Get out of my way,' I told him. 'Or I'll take you down, and Oriax will have to go begging for a vessel somewhere else.'

'James,' said the Indian kid, 'she's just a girl, and I can see the benefactors leaving. Shouldn't we ...'

'No,' Armstrong said, lunging left and right to bar me from getting out. 'Nothing can stop me. He won't let you stop me!'

'Give it up, James,' I snapped, raising my rapier, ready to try to strike him somewhere non-vital if I had to. 'I know Oriax. Whatever you've been offered, it isn't worth it!'

I realised I'd said the wrong thing as Armstrong shoved the Superman kid aside and lunged for me. I hesitated to bring up my rapier, not wanting to run him through, and my foot hit a patch of gasoline. I slipped and fell back into the smoke, hitting the wooden floor on my back with Armstrong on top of me, clumsily grabbing for my arms. I brought around an elbow and felt it connect, but the smoke was so thick I didn't know if I'd got him on the chin or the nose or the shoulder.

I tried to drag in a lungful of air, but it was pure smoke, and I gagged and choked, sparks dancing behind my eyes. For a terrifying moment I thought I would choke to death right here. In the distance, I could hear Armstrong, speaking with no trouble, as if the air was perfectly clear.

'You don't know anything about what he's offering me,' he growled. I could feel his hands fumbling for something.

My brain caught up. *It's me. The sacrifice is going to be* me. *GET UP!*

I bunched every muscle in my torso and threw myself forwards into the world's most painful sit-up. Armstrong lost balance and fell backwards. I heard something clatter on to the wooden floor.

Then his hands were around my neck, squeezing clumsily. He wasn't on my windpipe, but I still winced in pain and tried to head-butt him.

'You won't stop me!' he yelled. 'I won't let you stop me! I have to save my dad!'

'*Huh?*' I managed to grunt, as I worked my hands up between his, and fumbled for the angle on his fingers that I knew would break his grip.

'My dad's *dead*,' Armstrong said. 'He let my bitch stepmother get under his skin and he drove into a lake and now he's *dead* and I'm not going to let you or a *thousand* stupid girls stop me from bringing him back! Now *DIE!*'

Oh, kid.

Nothing was worth burning two hundred innocent people for, nothing – but if there was a list of runners-up, that sad story had to be pretty near the top.

I didn't have the breath to pity him out loud. I finally hooked my thumbs around his little fingers and bent them back hard. His grip broke and I shoved him off me. *Not today, sorry.*

'Oriax,' Armstrong sniffled. 'Help me! I want to do your work *but I don't know how ...*'

I jumped at the sound of his voice, dizzy with fear and the lack of air. There was another sound in the background when he spoke, now. It was the screech of death's-head moths. I scrambled to my feet and backed towards the faint light coming from the doorway, when a hissing sound made me spin around, rapier trembling but ready. Then I realised that there was water falling on me, spattering through the smoke.

The sprinklers had turned on.

'Oh my God,' gasped Minerva, as she appeared at my side. 'Diana, are you all right?'

'No. It's Oriax,' I said, blinking through the smoke and falling water, scraping my damp hair back from my face. 'It's here.'

The fire by the hall doors was dying down, and the smoke was being beaten back by the flow of water and escaping through the door behind us. I took a few experimentally deep breaths and we stepped forward, weapons raised, as a small blond figure was slowly revealed in the middle of the room, smoke curling around his feet.

'Flank him?' Minerva muttered.

I nodded. 'If we can get James in the net, we ...'

But as Minerva and Vesta carefully moved through the hall, trying not to trip on the ropes or slip on the mingling water and gasoline, James opened his mouth and laughed.

'*This one invited me in some time ago*,' he said – or *something* said. James's face, which had been twisted in anger and desperation and grief, had gone still now.

'Oriax,' I snarled. 'Get out of that boy, or we'll force you out.'

James/Oriax laughed again, and I shivered and

209

touched the back of my neck as the *skree skree skree* of the death's-head moths echoed in his voice. *'You understand nothing, even now. I have not been idle all these days. Let me show you.'*

Armstrong's head tipped back – and back, and back, until his mouth was pointed straight up at the ceiling. His jaw opened, wider than any human jaw should, and a stream of black shot out. It fluttered in a screeching cloud between the jets of water from the sprinklers.

'He's manifesting!' Minerva gasped. 'Why is he doing that?'

Armstrong crumpled to the wet floor, and Oriax's moths began to settle, landing and condensing down into a pair of legs, a torso with a red mouth right in the centre, moth wings and two pairs of arms.

I stared, trying to work out why it was doing this – but there was no time for that.

'Get it!' I yelled. 'Get into position!'

Vesta and Minerva splashed through the water to their positions, but Oriax's chest-mouth opened and it let out another *skree skree skree-hee* sound.

It was laughing again, but this time there was no human voice, only the screeching of the moths.

It held up a clawed hand and thrust it forwards – and the hand vanished. It twisted its arm, as if gripping and pulling something, and then ...

The air tore, not creating a puncture like the pinprick from below the Pont d'Iéna, but a huge, nasty rip, like skin caught on an old nail. Through the gap, I could see red and black earth, jutting rocks ...

And other, more horrible shapes. They clambered through the tear and into our world, mandibles clicking, tongues lolling, clawed fingers flexing.

The demons were coming.

CHAPTER SIXTEEN

The demons were all smaller than Oriax or the Dragon, but that didn't stop me from metaphorically crapping my pants as they tumbled out through the gap in reality. A yellow one was all teeth, sticking out at odd angles as if it had been turned inside out. A blue one with three arms leered at me with too-nearly-human blue eyes and panted like a dog. A black one lurched around on its knuckles, like a monkey, and opened its mouth to reveal a dozen pairs of chittering mandibles, arranged in rows like a shark's teeth.

Minerva slithered into position on the wet wood, and I felt my spine straighten. Power was crackling between us. We had them. If we stayed in formation, we could hold them here, prevent them ever getting out into the world beyond the school ...

But holding them here wasn't good enough.

We had to kill them. And we couldn't do that without moving.

I thrust my rapier at the eye of one of the smaller demons and it rolled away and hissed like a cat. Minerva had her bow out and was firing into the crowd of horrible creatures. She set an arrow that was crackling with lightning.

'Minerva, don't shock the water!' I shrieked.

'Or set fire to the gasoline!' Vesta added, swiping her kitchen knife through the air.

Minerva looked at the lightning in her hands and then at me, horror on her face.

'Thank you!' she said as she pressed the arrow between her hands, putting out the electricity.

Vesta was slicing at any demon that came near, but mostly they were simply gathering around Oriax's feet, circling it like dogs, ready to charge as soon as we made a move and dropped the net of power.

Behind me the door banged open. I heard feet splash into the room and stop, and heavy breathing.

'Oh,' Alex gasped. 'No ... no, no, what – what happened?'

I shook my head. 'Alex. Listen to me. Shut the doors and bolt them,' I told him. 'We can't let them out of here!'

I heard the sound of the doors slamming, and Alex throwing back the deadlocks.

Then I felt him take my empty hand. My heart juddered with confusion, and then with hope.

He'd pressed a long kitchen knife into my hand. He had one too.

It wasn't much. But it was an edged weapon, and in theory that was all I needed.

Before he could pull away, I hooked my little finger around his and held on tight for a second as the demons prowled and chittered in front of me, feeling the warmth of his hand in mine.

'Thanks,' I said, and dropped it again.

'So what's the plan?' he asked, standing back, readying himself.

'The plan?' Vesta said. 'The plan is ... kill them all.'

Alex rolled his shoulders. 'Good plan.'

'On three, then,' said Vesta. 'One. *Die!*' She leaped out of the formation, knife drawn back.

I laughed slightly hysterically at her, even as the power between us faded. The demon closest to her, a thin and wispy grey thing about her height, had completely fallen for the childish trick. It tried to raise its tentacular arms, but it was too late. Vesta had sunk her knife into the side of its neck, bearing it down to the ground. With a couple of splashes, she chopped its head clean off. Grey matter started to shred down and flow back towards the portal.

I spun forwards, slashing with the kitchen knife in one hand and stabbing with the rapier in the other. One of the smallest demons took a flying leap on to my leg and bared its teeth. I yelled and shook it off just before it bit down – I did not like the look of the green and red-flecked spittle dripping from its fangs.

Oriax roared its thousand-shrieking-moths roar and leaped for me. I ducked out of the way of its clawed hands and brought my rapier around to thrust into its side. Oriax barely seemed to register the wound. It spun to face me and I parried another face-full of claws with the kitchen knife. One of them caught me across the forehead. It stung, and I felt hot blood start to run down one side of my face.

Alex skidded forwards, and with a cry of rage like a wild animal he drove his knife deep into Oriax's chest, again and again.

'Alex!' I gasped. Every stab was loaded with fear and fury, but his trauma and vengeance were blinding him – he wasn't going for the neck. Too late, he realised his mistake and tried to slice at the demon's throat, but his hands were shaking too much and he missed.

One of Oriax's four hands seized him by the neck. Alex's eyes turned dark with terror. I leaped, driving my kitchen knife down through the demon's arm. It cut straight through and Alex fell back, crashing to the floor with Oriax's severed forearm beside him.

'Get back,' I said, helping Alex to his feet. 'Keep away from it.'

'I can't,' Alex snarled, his voice trembling. We both dived aside as Oriax flailed out in our direction with its three remaining hands. 'I can't, it has to die.'

'It *will*,' I told him, grabbing the back of his neck in what I hoped was a steadying gesture even though I was holding a long and sticky rapier in the same hand. 'I swear it. Go help Minerva.'

I released Alex, and he finally backed away.

Minerva was pinning the small demons to the ground with her arrows, and then yanking them back out so she could fire them again, but she was surrounded. Demons tore at her clothes and tried to knock her down.

Alex skidded across the wet floor and bowled into them, chopping left and right.

I dodged Oriax again, backing away in search of high ground, staring at what passed for its neck, trying to plot the move that would get me past its wicked-sharp claws.

'V, Di,' Minerva gasped. 'Look!'

Another figure was climbing out of the demon-world portal. It had long grey hair in a tight, blood-matted braid, and it was armed to the teeth, each one of the blades slung across its back and chest gleaming with a sticky oil-slick substance.

Isobel leaped from the portal with a scream and drew two curved swords across the neck of the closest demon, decapitating it before it even had time to turn and see her.

'Isobel!' all three of us chorused. She took a fighting stance and looked up, her eyes wild.

'On your right, Diana!' she cried, and I turned and drove my rapier up through the place that Oriax's chin should have been, if that thing on top of its shoulders was even really its head. That got a reaction, anyway: Oriax roared from its chest-mouth and spat a stream of moths at me. I vaulted over the receptionist's desk and hunkered down behind it while the moths whirled above my head.

Perhaps with Isobel here, we could actually win this fight!

But ... perhaps we *couldn't*.

We *needed* to kill them all. And we needed some way to hold them back. And we couldn't do both at the same time. We needed ...

At that moment, Vesta screamed. I jumped up, my heart thundering, to stand on the desk. The small demon with the dripping fangs had climbed up her back and sunk its teeth inches deep into her shoulder. Minerva let an arrow fly, and it shot straight and true across the hall and pierced the head of the demon, knocking it back off Vesta. As its fangs withdrew, I saw a stream of blood and something sickly green well up from the wounds and spill down Vesta's arm.

Vesta staggered, turned, and hacked at the demon, chopping off its head in a series of clumsy swipes. Then she gripped her shoulder, let out a wail of agony, lost her footing in the slick water and fell.

'V!' Minerva gasped. 'No, Vesta!'

Vesta tried to sit up, but the side where she'd been bitten seemed to be hanging heavy, too heavy even for her. She tore the remains of her white waitress shirt from her shoulder.

The skin was turning black.

Isobel skidded across the room to her side and tried to look at the wound, but as soon as she touched it Vesta screamed again.

I stood on the reception desk and looked down at the carnage, the rainbow of revolting flesh floating on the surface of the water, the smoke stains on the walls. Alex and Minerva fighting back to back. Isobel getting up and standing between Vesta and Oriax.

We needed to take control. And we couldn't. With Vesta down, with the demon portal open ... we couldn't.

But perhaps someone else could.

'Alex!' I yelled. 'Throw me your phone!'

'What?' Alex shouted back. But he fished in his pocket, and he threw me his mobile. I caught it in one hand, and groped in my own trouser pocket. There was a crumpled sheet of paper there.

Oriax took another swipe at Isobel, but she was standing her ground. A demon like an enormous yellow centipede was undulating across the floor towards Minerva and Alex, giant mandibles chomping.

I fumbled Henrietta's number into Alex's phone and hit *call*.

'Henrietta, are the others there?' I asked, as soon as they'd picked up.

'*Err ... qua? Diana, is this you? Yes, they are both here.*'

'Reach out your hand.'

'*Diana ...*'

'Vesta's hurt. We're getting killed here. I need you, Henrietta. Put out your hand!'

'*All right, I am ...*'

I shut my eyes, and just as Eva's instructions had said, I tried to block out the screams and the chittering and the smell of smoke and blood, and I held Henrietta's face in my mind. I imagined them, their whole self, as clearly as I could. Then I put out my hand.

Fingers brushed mine. I grabbed them, and I felt a sensation like being on a rollercoaster going backwards.

There were three high-pitched, Gallic-sounding yelps and a splash.

I opened my eyes.

A thin, shimmering line of light hung in the air in front of me – and the three Paris Demon Hunters lay sprawled on the floor in front of the desk.

'*Oh merde . . . Qu'est qui se passe*?!' Francine gasped, clambering to her feet and turning on the spot.

'We're going to destroy Oriax,' I said. 'But we need your help.'

CHAPTER SEVENTEEN

Two Trinities. It made so much sense that I kind of hated myself for not thinking of it before. I stood on the desk, surveying the scene, feeling like a general who could suddenly see a break in the enemy lines.

'Paris, get in formation, as wide as you can,' I called down.

None of the French Demon Hunters needed to be told twice. Henrietta floated above the slippery floor, their coat billowing, while Coralie flashed across the room and caught herself on the wall. Francine ran to Vesta. I saw the tears in her eyes as she looked down at the blackness creeping across Vesta's flesh, but I blocked it out.

Not yet. Nothing you can do now – except win.

'Alex, look after Henrietta,' I shouted. 'Minerva, take Coralie. Isobel, stay with Vesta and Franci.'

If Great-Aunt Isobel, ancient Demon Hunter, minded being ordered about then she didn't say so. She tossed her sword aside and drew out a short whip with a terrifyingly sharp-looking arrow point on the end, whirling it around in front of her, as if daring any demon to try to get to Vesta through it.

The yellow centipede demon reared up on a dozen pairs of legs and tried to lunge for Minerva as she ran to Coralie, but that was just the opening that Alex and Henrietta needed to take it down. Henrietta seized a metal shield that'd been hung high on the wall and flung it, so that it struck right in the centre of the centipede's long body. It twitched and went stiff, and Alex hacked at it until the top couple of segments were severed from the rest, and it finally went limp and started to disintegrate.

Oriax meanwhile spun on the spot, wading in the heads and limbs of its demon compatriots. Its expression was a torn-up vision of unreadable insectoid horror, but if I had to guess, I thought it would be confusion. Possibly even dismay.

It was surrounded. It had been fighting three humans, and suddenly there were eight.

And now the Paris Trinity stepped into formation, and Oriax screamed and writhed as it felt itself constrained.

'We've *got* you, you piece of shit,' I snarled, and took a flying leap off the desk and on to the demon's back.

The moment I crossed the Trinity's power threshold, I felt a strength I'd never known before. I knew what I had to do. I sank the rapier into Oriax's spine, or where the spine would have been on something real, and I used the sword's hilt as a handle to keep my hold on the demon as it bucked and tried to shake me off, its fluttering moth wings beating desperately, lifting us both off the floor.

I could feel its skin vibrating underneath me, crawling with the urge to split into a thousand shrieking moths and fly off again – but not this time. I grabbed a handful of its flesh and I opened my mind, but instead of it getting inside my head, I was inside *it*, holding it together, forbidding the moths to fly away.

And after that it was simple – disgusting, but simple. I hacked and hacked and hacked at the place where its neck probably was until the head came off in my hands and the rest of Oriax crashed to the ground.

I rolled off, splashing in the puddles, and for a moment everything was perfectly still. I got to my knees and looked up. Oriax's flesh was shredding – not into moths, but into the same thin, dead demon soup that the Dragon had turned into. The demon portal was sucking its own back in. Streams of coloured flesh-stuff rose from the water, past me, pouring back into its own world.

I sat back, looked up at Alex, and grinned.

Then Vesta let out a sob, and my blood ran cold.

The Paris Trinity dropped their formation and we all began to gather around her.

'You can fix it,' Minerva said. 'You can, right, Isobel?' She sank down by her twin's side and cradled her head, her face streaked with tears. The black stain was beginning to creep up over Vesta's neck. Vesta looked up at Minerva, opening and closing her cracked lips, but she couldn't speak.

Isobel's eyes were wild. 'I – perhaps – if I had – but there's no time.'

'Oh God,' I said, and dropped the knife, my hands coming up to cover my mouth. 'No, Vesta …'

I felt an arm across my shoulders, and looked up to see Henrietta standing behind me. They gathered me into their arms and I let myself be gathered.

Bang! Bang bang bang!

Every one of us jumped, Vesta too, as the noise reverberated around the hall.

'Hey!' came a familiar voice. 'Are you alive in there?'

'Oh God,' I said again.

It was Sebastian.

'S … Seb …' Vesta managed.

Coralie was at the door in a split second. She dragged back the heavy bolts and pulled open the door.

Sebastian slid on the wet floor, caught himself, stared at Coralie, at the sticky, smoke-stained carnage that had been the reception hall, and then his gaze landed on Vesta lying prone in Minerva's arms and he started forward.

But he slipped, and before he could right himself another two people ran past him, steadier on their feet.

One of them was John Yao. The other one was a girl, about seventeen, also Chinese. Did John Yao have a daughter?

She was carrying a large bag.

I held my breath and squeezed Henrietta's hands tight, hardly daring to hope. The bag clinked as the girl put it down. She opened it up, and inside I saw … substances. Things in jars. Syringes. *Bandages.*

Oh God, please. Please.

Nobody spoke as John and the girl got to work. Sebastian finally reached Vesta's side and we parted to let him get close. He stroked her wet, bloodied hair and held Minerva's hand.

Minerva looked up, her eyes blurred with tears, and saw the Chinese girl spreading something white across Vesta's puncture wound. She stared, as if she couldn't quite process what was happening. The girl's focus was intense as she splashed some clear liquid from a bottle on to Vesta's shoulder and began to rub it with a towel, but after another breathless minute she sat back and pulled the towel away, dripping with black gore.

Vesta's shoulder was clean. I could feel it radiating heat from where I stood, but the advance of the black stain had been stopped.

The girl looked up at Minerva, who was shaking like a leaf, and bit her lip. I saw her reach across, without speaking, and take Minerva's trembling hand from Sebastian.

Isobel was the one who finally spoke. 'John,' she said. 'Please tell me . . . '

John looked at the girl. 'Jennie?'

'Yes,' said the girl, in a San Francisco accent to match John's. 'I think she's going to be OK.'

Everybody breathed again, filling the vaunted room with a ghostly chorus of gasps and sighs.

'So, John Yao,' Isobel said. 'It's been a long time since I've spoken to one of your family in the flesh. They sent you for the girls, did they?' She gave him a long, thoughtful look. 'Good,' she finished.

Vesta stirred. She took in a deep breath and let it out as a long string of inventive curse words.

'Oh my God, V,' Minerva sobbed and hugged her sister tight.

'Lemme up. Wanna ... iss wet down here. Annit smells.'

'All right,' said Jennie. 'But *carefully*. You, boyfriend, take the other shoulder.'

Tears of happiness were streaking down Sebastian's face as he nodded and shifted so that between them, he and Minerva could get Vesta on to her feet.

'Girls, this is my daughter Jennie,' said John Yao. 'She's also coming to live here with me – I hope that's all right,' he added. 'I know we didn't get off on quite the right note, but you should be glad that Sebastian decided to fetch me when he did. Without Jennie ... ' he trailed off.

'Nice to meet you,' croaked Vesta, when she was on Jennie's eye-level. 'Cheers very much for saving my life.'

'No problem,' said Jennie cheerfully. Her gaze slid from Vesta's face back to Minerva's. 'So if you're Vesta, *you* must be Minerva?'

Minerva stared at Jennie. She blinked, and said, 'Er, I must be. Yes. I mean, I, sorry, I am, yes.'

'And so you're Diana.' Jennie turned to me, and we shook hands.

'And these are ... some friends of ours who I think it would be better to introduce back at home,' I said, gesturing around to the Paris Trinity and to Alex, and to Isobel ...

Isobel. She was here with us again, as if she'd come back from the dead.

Except ... she had never been dead. If I'd ever doubted that, here was the evidence: the scratches and bruises across her wrinkled face and hands, the chipped and broken blade of one of her swords, the blood and demon matter that coated her hair.

She was alive. She'd been fighting all this time, but she was alive, and she was planning to stay that way. I saw her glance over her shoulder, towards the tear in the world.

'You have to go again, don't you?' I said softly. Isobel turned to me. 'Couldn't you stay, just for ...'

I trailed off as Isobel gave me a stern look. 'There is an open portal to the demon world, in the front hall of ... is this some sort of school?'

'It's Wallington,' said Sebastian.

'Ha! The front hall of Scotland's most prestigious boarding school. No, Diana, I cannot stay, for any length of time.' Her expression softened, and she reached up to pat my cheek with one elderly hand. 'But it means a great deal that you would ask anyway.'

I ran to her and threw my arms around her neck. 'Thank you,' I said. 'Thank you for everything. And for everything you said in the letter. And for ... for *everything*.'

Isobel squeezed me hard and then pulled away to hug Minerva and Vesta and Sebastian.

I stood there, turning the knife I was still holding in my hands.

I could ask her about Mom. I could ask her now, before she goes away forever. Even if it would be selfish to make her talk about that when she was saying goodbye for the second and almost certainly final time.

'Isobel, can I ask you something?' I said, before I could talk myself out of it. She looked at me and took my hand.

'Quickly, Diana,' she said – about the most *Isobel* way she could possibly have responded.

'I need to know ... did you ever forgive my mom for leaving? You don't have to talk about it if you don't want to,' I blurted.

'Oh, Diana.' Isobel patted my hand. 'I knew you would ask me one day. I loved Kara *so much* ... it took me a long time to forgive her. I think if you asked me last week, I might have said no. But the truth is, if I resented her choice, it was because she was *family*. It hurt that she chose a life away from us over ... over her duty, but also over her love for me. I realise now that no matter how important, the choice *had* to be her own. *I* was the selfish one, not Kara. She chose to leave everything she knew, for a chance at a happy life. I think it may be the bravest thing I've ever seen.' She smiled. 'One day, Diana, you will be an old woman with a flock of Demon Hunter children in your care. Then, I believe, you will understand. Does that answer your question?'

I swallowed back my tears and nodded, utterly unable to speak. Isobel gathered Vesta, Minerva, Sebastian and me into a rather sticky, smelly group hug.

'I made the right choice,' she said, when we had relaxed our grip enough for her to get out of the hug again. 'But I'm very glad I got to see you all. One last time.'

'Hey, Isobel,' said Vesta, leaning on Minerva's shoulder. Isobel's eyebrows raised. 'Yes?'

I could see Vesta wrestling with herself, and for a

moment I thought she might break into exhausted sobs. But finally, she grinned weakly. 'Give 'em hell.'

'I will,' said Isobel. 'Goodbye, my dears.' She turned, squared her shoulders, and stepped into the tear.

There was no scream, this time – just a wavering in the air, a strange twist of perspective, and then the rip filled up with light, and ... was gone.

We stood in silence for a long moment, before we heard the wail of sirens.

'That'll be the police and the fire brigade,' said John. 'I suggest that all of us are elsewhere when they get here.'

'I'm going to stay,' said Alex's voice. 'With James.'

I turned to see Alex standing with a bedraggled but conscious James Armstrong.

'Someone has to try to explain what happened here. James set fire to the building. He's going to need someone to make sure they treat him fairly.'

'Really?' Vesta raised an eyebrow. But I caught her eye and shook my head.

James was shaking like a child in the grip of a bout of pneumonia. He was crying.

If I could kill a handful of strangers to bring my mother back from the dead, would I do it? No, absolutely not.

But if a demon had offered me that power six months after she had died, when the wound was still raw, and the pain seemed like it would never end, and I was just a frightened, angry child and the world had proven beyond doubt that it was a cruel, unfair place?

I hoped the answer was still no. But I was also glad I didn't have to find out for sure.

'All right, come on, let's be away from here before we end up having to explain ourselves,' said John, ushering everyone out into the star-dusted night.

I gave Alex a smile and turned to follow them. Then I heard Alex speaking.

'Listen to me,' he said softly, and I knew he was talking to James. 'I don't know what's going to happen now. You did some very bad things. *You* did them. But I ... I know something about losing people, and losing yourself. Oriax was with you, steering you as hard as he could, but even then, you never did kill anybody. You hear me? *You are not a murderer.*'

James let out a sniffling sob.

Something in my heart went *twang*.

I turned on my heel. I walked up to Alex, and I put both my hands firmly on his chest, stepping close, closer than we had been since we'd danced and kissed, that night when he wasn't responsible for his actions ...

'*You*,' I said. 'You ... come to Isobel's when you're done here. Don't vanish again. I don't care what time it is. Come find me.'

Alex paused, taking a breath that lifted my hands. His eyes shone, and he nodded. He reached up and very gently touched my hair, right at the temple. Then he swallowed and pulled back. 'I'll see you later,' he said.

'You will,' I said, and smiled at him. 'Believe me. You are gonna see a lot of me.'

I turned and hurried away before he could see me flushing red. I caught up with the others as they were piling into Ruby, and into John Yao's car, in the parking lot.

Vesta was still draped across Minerva's shoulders, but she was already standing up a little straighter. She was also giving her sister an intense *I know something you don't know* kind of grin.

Minerva was watching the Paris Trinity climb into John Yao's car with a faraway look on her face. Jennie Yao stuck her head out of the car window and smiled at her. 'See you back at the house, Minerva,' she said. 'Don't let Sebastian take any sharp corners with Vesta in the back.'

'I – I – I won't,' Minerva said. Jennie settled back behind the windshield and Minerva suddenly turned to Vesta. '... huh, what? What did you just say?'

'I didn't say a thing,' Vesta smirked. 'Jennie's nice, isn't she? Did you notice that the floor's on fire?'

'She seems ...' Minerva said, and then trailed off. For a second the only sound was the still-far-off wail of approaching sirens. 'Wait, what? The floor what?'

'I said the floor's on fire, dummy,' Vesta waggled her eyebrows at her sister.

'No it—' Minerva said, looking down. Then her face went beetroot red and she glared at her twin. 'Oh my God. Vesta. *Stop.*'

'*Never*, Miss "Aggressively heterosexual", Miss "Were you thinking about Sebastian in the shower?",' said Vesta.

'Wait, what?' said Sebastian.

'Revenge, at last!' Vesta went on.

'Just so you know, I'm going to tell this story at your wedding,' I agreed.

Minerva glared at both of us. 'I hate you. Don't you

230

dare say anything to her! Don't think I won't kick your arse, just because you nearly died.'

I took a deep, steadying breath of the fresh night air, and then I tackled both of them into a hug. 'I love you idiots so freaking much,' I said.

We all climbed into Ruby, and Sebastian eased us out of the Wallington gates and away, taking a selection of tiny lanes and strange turnings – as gently as he could – until the sirens had passed us, and we were on our way home.

I twisted in the front seat to look back at Minerva and Vesta. They'd gone quiet. Vesta's face was pale as she leaned on her sister's shoulder with her eyes closed and a smug smile playing across her lips. She reached up, around the driver's headrest, and touched her fingertips gently to the base of Sebastian's neck.

Sebastian let out a happy but strangled yelp.

'Don't do that; do you want him to crash the car?' Minerva said, batting her sister's hand away gently.

'So much more kissing,' said Vesta, her eyes still closed. Was she flirting in her sleep? Sebastian was as red as Ruby's paint job, but he was grinning.

Minerva reached up and ran her fingers through her hair, and then smiled out of the window into the dark, laughing at herself, maybe seeing something in the reflection, or in her imagination, that she hadn't seen before.

Oriax was dead, and so was *le Dragon Rouge*. I felt a burst of pride, and a tiny flicker of fear. If demons were bursting through the fabric of reality all by themselves, we were going to have work to do, and it wasn't going to be easy.

But I didn't need it to be easy. After all, we'd lost Isobel, but I understood her choice. We'd nearly lost Vesta, but she was still with us. And we'd gained so much – Eva, Henrietta, Cora and Francine. John and Jennie. And Alex.

Sebastian turned us back on to the main road, and I settled back in my seat and let the sight of Edinburgh's rooftops rising up to meet us fill my mind and my heart. At home there would be Dad, a bath, toast, friends, sleep. That would be good. But some part of me would always be right here – riding in Ruby, covered in blood and muck and sweat, my limbs aching. With Vesta, Minerva and Sebastian, trundling down the hill towards the twinkling lights of Edinburgh, ready to face whatever the world would throw at us next.